RAY BRADBURY is one of the greatest writers of fantasy and horror fiction in the world today. His stories have been translated into innumerable foreign languages and many of them have been adapted successfully for television and the cinema. Among his world-bestselling titles are *The Silver Locusts* (1950), (*The Martian Chronicles*) and *Fahrenheit 451* (1951).

'Ray Bradbury has a powerful and mysterious imagination which would undoubtedly earn the respect of Edgar Allan Poe' *The Guardian*.

Ray Bradbury

The Illustrated Man

Panther

Granada Publishing Limited
Published in 1977 by Panther Books Ltd
Frogmore, St Albans, Herts AL2 2NF

First published in Great Britain by
Rupert Hart-Davis Ltd 1952
Copyright © Ray Bradbury 1952
Made and printed in Great Britain by
Cox & Wyman Ltd, London, Reading and Fakenham
Set in Intertype Plantin

CONTENTS

PROLOGUE:
THE ILLUSTRATED MAN

*It was a warm afternoon in early September when I first met
the Illustrated Man. Walking along an asphalt road, I was on
the final leg of a two weeks' walking tour of Wisconsin. Late in
the afternoon I stopped, ate some pork, beans, and a doughnut,
and was preparing to stretch out and read when the Illustrated
Man walked over the hill and stood for a moment against the
sky.*

*I didn't know he was Illustrated then, I only knew that he
was tall, once well muscled, but now, for some reason, going to
fat. I recall that his arms were long, and the hands thick, but
that his face was like a child's, set upon a massive body.*

*He seemed only to sense my presence, for he didn't look
directly at me when he spoke his first words:*

'Do you know where I can find a job?'

'I'm afraid not,' I said.

'I haven't had a job that's lasted in forty years,' he said.

*Though it was a hot late afternoon, he wore his wool shirt
buttoned tight about his neck. His sleeves were rolled and buttoned down over his thick wrists. Perspiration was streaming
from his face, yet he made no move to open his shirt.*

*'Well,' he said at last, 'this is as good a place as any to spend
the night. Do you mind company?'*

'I have some extra food you'd be welcome to,' I said.

*He sat down heavily, grunting. 'You'll be sorry you asked me
to stay,' he said. 'Everyone always is. That's why I'm walking.
Here it is, early September, the cream of the Labour Day carnival season. I should be making money hand over fist at any
small town sideshow celebration, but here I am with no
prospects.'*

*He took off an immense shoe and peered at it closely. 'I
usually keep a job about ten days. Then something happens and*

they fire me. By now every carnival in America won't touch me with a ten-foot pole.'

'What seems to be the trouble?' I asked.

For answer, he unbuttoned his tight collar, slowly. With his eyes shut, he put a slow hand to the task of unbuttoning his shirt all the way down. He slipped his fingers in to feel his chest. 'Funny,' he said, eyes still shut. 'You can't feel them but they're there. I always hope that someday I'll look and they'll be gone. I walk in the sun for hours on the hottest days, baking, and hope that my sweat'll wash them off, the sun'll cook them off, but at sundown they're still there.' He turned his head slightly toward me and exposed his chest. 'Are they still there now?'

After a long while I exhaled. 'Yes,' I said. 'They're still there.'

The Illustrations.

'Another reason I keep my collar buttoned up,' he said, opening his eyes, 'is the children. They follow me along country roads. Everyone wants to see the pictures, and yet nobody wants to see them.'

He took his shirt off and wadded it in his hands. He was covered with Illustrations from the blue tattooed ring about his neck to his belt line.

'It keeps right on going,' he said, guessing my thought. 'All of me is Illustrated. Look.' He opened his hand. On his palm was a rose, freshly cut, with drops of crystal water among the soft pink petals. I put my hand out to touch it, but it was only an Illustration.

As for the rest of him, I cannot say how I sat and stared, for he was a riot of rockets and fountains and people, in such intricate detail and colour that you could hear the voices murmuring small and muted, from the crowds that inhabited his body. When his flesh twitched, the tiny mouths flickered, the tiny green-and-gold eyes winked, the tiny pink hands gestured. There were yellow meadows and blue rivers and mountains and stars and suns and planets spread in a Milky Way across his chest. The people themselves were in twenty or more odd groups upon his arms, shoulders, back, sides, and wrists, as well *as on the flat of his stomach. You found them in forests of hair, lurking among a constellation of freckles, or peering from armpit caverns, diamond eyes aglitter. Each seemed intent upon his own activity; each was a separate gallery portrait.*

'Why, they're beautiful!' I said.

How can I explain about his Illustrations? If El Greco had painted miniatures in his prime, no bigger than your hand, infinitely detailed, with all his sulphurous colour, elongation, and anatomy, perhaps he might have used this man's body for his art. The colours burned in three dimensions. They were windows looking in upon fiery reality. Here, gathered on one wall, were all the finest scenes in the universe; the man was a walking treasure gallery. This wasn't the work of a cheap carnival tattoo man with three colours and whisky on his breath. This was the accomplishment of a living genius, vibrant, clear, and beautiful.

'Oh yes,' said the Illustrated Man. 'I'm so proud of my Illustrations that I'd like to burn them off. I've tried sandpaper, acid, a knife . . .'

The sun was setting. The moon was already up in the East.

'For, you see,' said the Illustrated Man, 'these Illustrations predict the future.'

I said nothing.

'It's all right in sunlight,' he went on. 'I could keep a carnival day job. But at night – the pictures move. The pictures change.'

I must have smiled. 'How long have you been Illustrated?'

'In 1900, when I was twenty years old and working a carnival, I broke my leg. It laid me up; I had to do something to keep my hand in, so I decided to get tattooed.'

'But who tattooed you? What happened to the artist?'

'She went back to the future,' he said. 'I mean it. She was an old woman in a little house in the middle of Wisconsin here somewhere not far from this place. A little old witch who looked a thousand years old one moment and twenty years old the next, but she said she could travel in time. I laughed. Now, I know better.'

'How did you happen to meet her?'

He told me. He had seen her painted sign by the road: SKIN

ILLUSTRATION! *Illustration instead of tattoo! Artistic! So he had sat all night while her magic needles stung him wasp stings and delicate bee stings. By morning he looked like a man who had fallen into a twenty-colour printing press and been squeezed out, all bright and picturesque.*

'I've hunted every summer for fifty years,' he said, putting his hands out on the air. 'When I find that witch I'm going to kill her.'

The sun was gone. Now the first stars were shining and the moon had brightened the fields of grass and wheat. Still the Illustrated Man's pictures glowed like charcoals in the half light, like scattered rubies and emeralds, with Rouault colours and Picasso colours and the long, pressed-out El Greco bodies.

'So people fire me when my pictures move. They don't like it when violent things happen in my Illustrations. Each Illustration is a little story. If you watch them, in a few minutes they tell you a tale. In three hours of looking you could see eighteen or twenty stories acted right on my body, you could hear voices and think thoughts. It's all here, just waiting for you to look. But most of all, there's a special spot on my body.' He bared his back. 'See? There's no special design on my right shoulder-blade, just a jumble.'

'Yes.'

'When I've been around a person long enough, that spot clouds over and fills in. If I'm with a woman, her picture comes there on my back, in an hour, and shows her whole life – how she'll live, how she'll die, what she'll look like when she's sixty. And if it's a man, an hour later his picture's here on my back. It shows him falling off a cliff, or dying under a train. So I'm fired again.'

All the time he had been talking his hands had wandered over the Illustrations, as if to adjust their frames, to brush away dust – the motions of a connoisseur, an art patron. Now he lay back, long and full in the moonlight. It was a warm night. There was no breeze and the air was stifling. We both had our shirts off.

'And you've never found the old woman?'

'Never.'

'And you think she came from the future?'

'How else could she know these stories she painted on me?'

He shut his eyes tiredly. His voice grew fainter. 'Sometimes at night I can feel them, the pictures, like ants, crawling on my skin. Then I know they're doing what they have to do. I never look at them any more. I just try to rest. I don't sleep much. Don't you look at them either, I warn you. Turn the other way when you sleep.'

I lay back a few feet from him. He didn't seem violent, and the pictures were beautiful. Otherwise I might have been tempted to get out and away from such babbling. But the Illustrations . . . I let my eyes fill up on them. Any person would go a little mad with such things upon his body.

The night was serene. I could hear the Illustrated Man's breathing in the moonlight. Crickets were stirring gently in the distant ravines. I lay with my body sidewise so I could watch the Illustrations. Perhaps half an hour passed. Whether the Illustrated Man slept I could not tell, but suddenly I heard him whisper, 'They're moving, aren't they?'

I waited a minute.

Then I said, 'Yes.'

The pictures were moving, each in its turn, each for a brief minute or two. There in the moonlight, with the tiny tinkling thoughts and the distant sea voices, it seemed, each little drama was enacted. Whether it took an hour or three hours for the dramas to finish, it would be hard to say. I only know that I lay fascinated and did not move while the stars wheeled in the sky.

Sixteen Illustrations, sixteen tales. I counted them one by one.

Primarily my eyes focused upon a scene, a large house with two people in it. I saw a flight of vultures on a blazing flesh sky, I saw yellow lions, and I heard voices.

The first Illustration quivered and came to life.

THE VELD

'George, I wish you'd look at the nursery.'

'What's wrong with it?'

'I don't know.'

'Well, then.'

'I just want you to look at it, is all, or call a psychologist in to look at it.'

'What would a psychologist want with a nursery?'

'You know very well what he'd want.' His wife paused in the middle of the kitchen and watched the stove busy humming to itself, making supper for four.

'It's just that the nursery is different now than it was.'

'All right, let's have a look.'

They walked down the hall of their sound-proofed, Happylife Home, which had cost them thirty thousand dollars installed, this house which clothed and fed and rocked them to sleep and played and sang and was good to them. Their approach sensitized a switch somewhere and the nursery light flicked on when they came within ten feet of it. Similarly, behind them, in the halls, lights went on and off as they left them behind, with a soft automaticity.

'Well,' said George Hadley.

They stood on the thatched floor of the nursery. It was forty feet across by forty feet long and thirty feet high, it had cost half again as much as the rest of the house. 'But nothing's too good for our children,' George had said.

The nursery was silent. It was empty as a jungle glade at hot high noon. The walls were blank and two-dimensional. Now, as George and Lydia Hadley stood in the centre of the room, the walls began to purr and recede into crystalline distance, it seemed, and presently an African veld appeared, in three dimensions, on all sides, in colour, reproduced to the final pebble and bit of straw. The ceiling above them became a deep sky with a hot yellow sun.

George Hadley felt the perspiration start on his brow.

'Let's get out of this sun,' he said. 'This is a little too real. But I don't see anything wrong.'

'Wait a moment, you'll see,' said his wife.

Now the hidden odorophonics were beginning to blow a wind of odour at the two people in the middle of the baked veldland. The hot straw smell of lion grass, the cool green smell of the hidden water hole, the great rusty smell of animals, the smell of dust like a red paprika in the hot air. And now the sounds: the thump of distant antelope feet on grassy sod, the papery rustling of vultures. A shadow passed through the sky. The shadow flickered on George Hadley's upturned, sweating face.

'Filthy creatures,' he heard his wife say.

'The vultures.'

'You see, there are the lions, far over, that way. Now they're on their way to the water hole. They've just been eating,' said Lydia. 'I don't know what.'

'Some animal.' George Hadley put his hand up to shield off the burning light from his squinted eyes. 'A zebra or a baby giraffe, maybe.'

'Are you *sure*?' His wife sounded peculiarly tense.

'No, it's a little late to be *sure*,' he said, amused. 'Nothing over there I can see but cleaned bone, and the vultures dropping for what's left.'

'Did you hear that scream?' she asked.

'No.'

'About a minute ago?'

'Sorry, no.'

The lions were coming. And again George Hadley was filled with admiration for the mechanical genius who had conceived this room. A miracle of efficiency selling for an absurdly low price. Every home should have one. Oh, occasionally they frightened you with their clinical accuracy, they startled you, gave you a twinge, but most of the time what fun for everyone, not only your own son and daughter, but for yourself when you felt like a quick jaunt to a foreign land, a quick change of scenery. Well, here it was!

And here were the lions now, fifteen feet away, so real, so feverishly and startlingly real that you could feel the prickling fur on your hand, and your mouth was stuffed with the dusty upholstery smell of their heated pelts, and the yellow of them was in your eyes like the yellow of an exquisite French tapestry, the yellows of lions and summer grass, and the sound of the matted lion lungs exhaling on the silent noontide, and the smell of meat from the panting, dripping mouths.

The lions stood looking at George and Lydia Hadley with terrible green-yellow eyes.

'Watch out!' screamed Lydia.

The lions came running at them.

Lydia bolted and ran. Instinctively, George sprang after her. Outside, in the hall, with the door slammed, he was laughing and she was crying, and they both stood appalled at the other's reaction.

'George!'

'Lydia! Oh, my dear poor sweet Lydia!'

'They almost got us!'

'Walls, Lydia, remember; crystal walls, that's all they are. Oh, they look real, I must admit – Africa in your parlour – but it's all dimensional super-reactionary, super-sensitive colour film and mental tape film behind glass screens. It's all odorophonics and sonics, Lydia. Here's my handkerchief.'

'I'm afraid.' She came to him and put her body against him and cried steadily. 'Did you see? Did you feel? It's too real.'

'Now, Lydia . . .'

'You've got to tell Wendy and Peter not to read any more on Africa.'

'Of course – of course.' He patted her.

'Promise?'

'Sure.'

'And lock the nursery for a few days until I get my nerves settled.'

'You know how difficult Peter is about that. When I punished him a month ago by locking the nursery for even a few hours – the tantrum he threw! And Wendy too. They live for the nursery.'

'It's got to be locked, that's all there is to it.'

'All right.' Reluctantly he locked the huge door. 'You've been working too hard. You need a rest.'

'I don't know – I don't know,' she said, blowing her nose, sitting down in a chair that immediately began to rock and comfort her. 'Maybe I don't have enough to do. Maybe I have time to think too much. Why don't we shut the whole house off for a few days and take a vacation?'

'You mean you want to fry my eggs for me?'

'Yes.' She nodded.

'And darn my socks?'

'Yes.' A frantic, watery-eyed nodding.

'And sweep the house?'

'Yes, yes – oh, yes!'

'But I thought that's why we bought this house, so we wouldn't have to do anything?'

'That's just it. I feel I don't belong here. The house is wife and mother now and nursemaid. Can I compete with an African veld? Can I give a bath and scrub the children as efficiently or quickly as the automatic scrub bath can? I cannot. And it isn't just me. It's you. You've been awfully nervous lately.'

'I suppose I have been smoking too much.'

'You look as if you didn't know what to do with yourself in this house, either. You smoke a little more every morning and drink a little more every afternoon and need a little more sedative every night. You're beginning to feel unnecessary too.'

'Am I?' He paused and tried to feel into himself to see what was really there.

'Oh, George!' She looked beyond him, at the nursery door. 'Those lions can't get out of there, can they?'

He looked at the door and saw it tremble as if something had jumped against it from the other side.

'Of course not,' he said.

At dinner they ate alone, for Wendy and Peter were at a special plastic carnival across town and had televised home to

say they'd be late, to go ahead eating. So George Hadley, bemused, sat watching the dining-room table produce warm
dishes of food from its mechanical interior.

'We forgot the ketchup,' he said.

'Sorry,' said a small voice within the table, and ketchup appeared.

As for the nursery, thought George Hadley, it won't hurt for
the children to be locked out of it awhile. Too much of anything
isn't good for anyone. And it was clearly indicated that the
children had been spending a little too much time on Africa.
That *sun*. He could feel it on his neck, still, like a hot paw. And
the *lions*. And the smell of blood. Remarkable how the nursery
caught the telepathic emanations of the children's minds and
created life to fill their every desire. The children thought lions,
and there were lions. The children thought zebras, and there
were zebras. Sun – sun. Giraffes – giraffes. Death and death.

That *last*. He chewed tastelessly on the meat that the table
had cut for him. Death thoughts. They were awfully young,
Wendy and Peter, for death thoughts. Or, no, you were never
too young, really. Long before you knew what death was you
were wishing it on someone else. When you were two years old
you were shooting people with cap pistols.

But this – the long, hot African veld – the awful death in the
jaws of a lion. And repeated again and again.

'Where are you going?'

He didn't answer Lydia. Preoccupied, he let the lights glow
softly on ahead of him, extinguish behind him as he padded to
the nursery door. He listened against it. Far away, a lion roared.

He unlocked the door and opened it. Just before he stepped
inside, he heard a far-away scream. And then another roar from
the lions, which subsided quickly.

He stepped into Africa. How many times in the last year had
he opened this door and found Wonderland, Alice, the Mock
Turtle, or Aladdin and his Magical Lamp, or Jack Pumpkinhead of Oz, or Dr. Doolittle, or the cow jumping over a very
real-appearing moon – all the delightful contraptions of a make-
believe world. How often had he seen Pegasus flying in the sky
ceiling, or seen fountains of red fireworks, or heard angel voices

singing. But now, this yellow hot Africa, this bake oven with murder in the heat. Perhaps Lydia was right. Perhaps they needed a little vacation from the fantasy which was growing a bit too real for ten-year-old children. It was all right to exercise one's mind with gymnastic fantasies, but when the lively child mind settled on one pattern . . . ? It seemed that, at a distance, for the past month, he had heard lions roaring, and smelled their strong odour seeping as far away as his study door. But, being busy, he had paid it no attention.

George Hadley stood on the African grassland alone. The lions looked up from their feeding, watching him. The only flaw to the illusion was the open door through which he could see his wife, far down the dark hall, like a framed picture, eating her dinner abstractedly.

'Go away,' he said to the lions.

They did not go.

He knew the principle of the room exactly. You sent out your thoughts. Whatever you thought would appear.

'Let's have Aladdin and his lamp,' he snapped.

The veldland remained, the lions remained.

'Come on, room! I demand Aladdin!' he said.

Nothing happened. The lions mumbled in their baked pelts.

'Aladdin!'

He went back to dinner. 'The fool room's out of order,' he said. 'It won't respond.'

'Or—'

'Or what?'

'Or it *can't* respond,' said Lydia, 'because the children have thought about Africa and lions and killing so many days that the room's in a rut.'

'Could be.'

'Or Peter's set it to remain that way.'

'*Set* it?'

'He may have got into the machinery and fixed something.'

'Peter doesn't know machinery.'

'He's a wise one for ten. That I.Q. of his—'

'Nevertheless—'

'Hello, Mom. Hello, Dad.'

The Hadleys turned. Wendy and Peter were coming in the front door, cheeks like peppermint candy, eyes like bright blue agate marbles, a smell of ozone on their jumpers from their trip in the helicopter.

'You're just in time for supper,' said both parents.

'We're full of strawberry ice cream and hot dogs,' said the children, holding hands. 'But we'll sit and watch.'

'Yes, come tell us about the nursery,' said George Hadley.

The brother and sister blinked at him and then at each other. 'Nursery?'

'All about Africa and everything,' said the father with false joviality.

'I don't understand,' said Peter.

'Your mother and I were just travelling through Africa with rod and reel; Tom Swift and his Electric Lion,' said George Hadley.

'There's no Africa in the nursery,' said Peter simply.

'Oh, come now, Peter. We know better.'

'I don't remember any Africa,' said Peter to Wendy. 'Do you?'

'No.'

'Run see and come tell.'

She obeyed.

'Wendy, come back here!' said George Hadley, but she was gone. The house lights followed her like a flock of fireflies. Too late, he realized he had forgotten to lock the nursery door after his last inspection.

'Wendy'll look and come tell us,' said Peter.

'She doesn't have to tell *me*, I've seen it.'

'I'm sure you're mistaken, Father.'

'I'm not, Peter. Come along now.'

But Wendy was back. 'It's not Africa,' she said breathlessly.

'We'll see about this,' said George Hadley, and they all walked down the hall together and opened the nursery door.

There was a green, lovely forest, a lovely river, a purple mountain, high voices singing, and Rima, lovely and mysterious, lurking in the trees with colourful flights of butterflies, like animated bouquets, lingering in her long hair. The African veldland was gone. The lions were gone. Only Rima was here now, singing a song so beautiful that it brought tears to your eyes.

George Hadley looked in at the changed scene. 'Go to bed,' he said to the children.

They opened their mouths.

'You heard me,' he said.

They went off to the air closet, where a wind sucked them like brown leaves up the flue to their slumber rooms.

George Hadley walked through the singing glade and picked up something that lay in the corner near where the lions had been. He walked slowly back to his wife.

'What is that?' she asked.

'An old wallet of mine,' he said.

He showed it to her. The smell of hot grass was on it and the smell of a lion. There were drops of saliva on it, it had been chewed, and there were blood smears on both sides.

He closed the nursery door and locked it, tight.

In the middle of the night he was still awake and he knew his wife was awake. 'Do you think Wendy changed it?' she said at last, in the dark room.

'Of course.'

'Made it from a veld into a forest and put Rima there instead of lions?'

'Yes.'

'Why?'

'I don't know. But it's staying locked until I find out.'

'How did your wallet get there?'

'I don't know anything,' he said, 'except that I'm beginning to be sorry we bought that room for the children. If children are neurotic at all, a room like that—'

'It's supposed to help them work off their neuroses in a healthful way.'

'I'm starting to wonder.' He stared at the ceiling.

'We've given the children everything they ever wanted. Is this our reward – secrecy, disobedience?'

'Who was it said, "Children are carpets, they should be stepped on occasionally"? We've never lifted a hand. They're insufferable – let's admit it. They come and go when they like; they treat us as if *we* were offspring. They're spoiled and we're spoiled.'

'They've been acting funny ever since you forbade them to take the rocket to New York a few months ago.'

'They're not old enough to do that alone, I explained.'

'Nevertheless, I've noticed they've been decidedly cool toward us since.'

'I think I'll have David McClean come tomorrow morning to have a look at Africa.'

'But it's not Africa now, it's Green Mansions country and Rima.'

'I have a feeling it'll be Africa again before then.'

A moment later they heard the screams.

Two screams. Two people screaming from downstairs. And then a roar of lions.

'Wendy and Peter aren't in their rooms,' said his wife.

He lay in his bed with his beating heart. 'No,' he said. 'They've broken into the nursery.'

'Those screams – they sound familiar.'

'Do they?'

'Yes, awfully.'

And although their beds tried very hard, the two adults couldn't be rocked to sleep for another hour. A smell of cats was in the night air.

'Father?' said Peter.

'Yes.'

Peter looked at his shoes. He never looked at his father any more, nor at his mother. 'You aren't going to lock up the nursery for good, are you?'

'That all depends.'

'On what?' snapped Peter.

'On you and your sister. If you intersperse this Africa with a little variety – oh, Sweden perhaps, or Denmark or China—'

'I thought we were free to play as we wished.'

'You are, within reasonable bounds.'

'What's wrong with Africa, Father?'

'Oh, so now you admit you have been conjuring up Africa, do you?'

'I wouldn't want the nursery locked up,' said Peter coldly. 'Ever.'

'Matter of fact, we're thinking of turning the whole house off for about a month. Live sort of a carefree one-for-all existence.'

'That sounds dreadful! Would I have to tie my own shoes instead of letting the shoe tier do it? And brush my own teeth and comb my hair and give myself a bath?'

'It would be fun for a change, don't you think?'

'No, it would be horrid. I didn't like it when you took out the picture painter last month.'

'That's because I wanted you to learn to paint all by yourself, son.'

'I don't want to do anything but look and listen and smell; what else is there to do?'

'All right, go play in Africa.'

'Will you shut off the house sometime soon?'

'We're considering it.'

'I don't think you'd better consider it any more, Father.'

'I won't have any threats from my son!'

'Very well.' And Peter strolled off to the nursery.

'Am I on time?' said David McClean.

'Breakfast?' asked George Hadley.

'Thanks, had some. What's the trouble?'

'David, you're a psychologist.'

'I should hope so.'

'Well, then, have a look at our nursery. You saw it a year ago when you dropped by; did you notice anything peculiar about it then?'

'Can't say I did; the usual violences, a tendency toward a slight paranoia here or there, usual in children because they feel persecuted by parents constantly, but, oh, really nothing.'

They walked down the hall. 'I locked the nursery up,' explained the father, 'and the children broke back into it during the night. I let them stay so they could form the patterns for you to see.'

There was a terrible screaming from the nursery.

'There it is,' said George Hadley. 'See what you make of it.'

They walked in on the children without rapping.

The screams had faded. The lions were feeding.

'Run outside a moment, children,' said George Hadley. 'No, don't change the mental combination. Leave the walls as they are. Get!'

With the children gone, the two men stood studying the lions clustered at a distance, eating with great relish whatever it was they had caught.

'I wish I knew what it was,' said George Hadley. 'Sometimes I can almost see. Do you think if I brought high-powered binoculars here and—'

David McClean laughed dryly. 'Hardly.' He turned to study all four walls. 'How long has this been going on?'

'A little over a month.'

'It certainly doesn't feel good.'

'I want facts, not feelings.'

'My dear George, a psychologist never saw a fact in his life. He only hears about feelings; vague things. This doesn't feel good, I tell you. Trust my hunches and my instincts, I have a nose for something bad. This is very bad. My advice to you is to have the whole damn room torn down and your children brought to me every day during the next year for treatment.'

'Is it that bad?'

'I'm afraid so. One of the original uses of these nurseries was so that we could study the patterns left on the walls by the child's mind, study at our leisure, and help the child. In this case, however, the room has become a channel toward – destructive thoughts, instead of a release away from them.'

'Didn't you sense this before?'

'I sensed only that you had spoiled your children more than most. And now you're letting them down in some way. What way?'

'I wouldn't let them go to New York.'

'What else?'

'I've taken a few machines from the house and threatened them, a month ago, with closing up the nursery unless they did their homework. I did close it for a few days to show I meant business.'

'Ah, ha!'

'Does that mean anything?'

'Everything. Where before they had a Santa Claus now they have a Scrooge. Children prefer Santas. You've let this room and this house replace you and your wife in your children's affections. This room is their mother and father, far more important in their lives than their real parents. And now you come along and want to shut it off. No wonder there's hatred here. You can feel it coming out of the sky. Feel that sun. George, you'll have to change your life. Like too many others, you've built it around creature comforts. Why, you'd starve tomorrow if something went wrong in your kitchen. You wouldn't know how to tap an egg. Nevertheless, turn everything off. Start new. It'll take time. But we'll make good children out of bad in a year, wait and see.'

'But won't the shock be too much for the children, shutting the room up abruptly, for good?'

'I don't want them going any deeper into this, that's all.'

The lions were finished with their red feast.

The lions were standing on the edge of the clearing watching the two men.

'Now *I'm* feeling persecuted,' said McClean. 'Let's get out of here. I never have cared for these damned rooms. Make me nervous.'

'The lions look real, don't they?' said George Hadley. 'I don't suppose there's any way—'

'What?'

'—that they could *become* real?'

'Not that I know.'

'Some flaw in the machinery, a tampering or something?'

'No.'

They went to the door.

'I don't imagine the room will like being turned off,' said the father.

'Nothing ever likes to die – even a room.'

'I wonder if it hates me for wanting to switch it off?'

'Paranoia is thick around here today,' said David McClean. 'You can follow it like a spoor. Hello.' He bent and picked up a bloody scarf. 'This yours?'

'No.' George Hadley's face was rigid. 'It belongs to Lydia.'

They went to the fuse box together and threw the switch that killed the nursery.

The two children were in hysterics. They screamed and pranced and threw things. They yelled and sobbed and swore and jumped at the furniture.

'You can't do that to the nursery, you can't!'

'Now, children.'

The children flung themselves on to a couch, weeping.

'George,' said Lydia Hadley, 'turn on the nursery, just for a few moments. You can't be so abrupt.'

'No.'

'You can't be so cruel.'

'Lydia, it's off, and it stays off. And the whole damn house dies as of here and now. The more I see of the mess we've put ourselves in, the more it sickens me. We've been contemplating our mechanical, electronic navels for too long. My God, how we need a breath of honest air!'

And he marched about the house turning off the voice clocks, the stoves, the heaters, the shoe shiners, the shoe lacers, the body scrubbers and swabbers and massagers, and every other machine he could put his hand to.

The house was full of dead bodies, it seemed. It felt like a mechanical cemetery. So silent. None of the humming hidden energy of machines waiting to function at the tap of a button.

'Don't let them do it!' wailed Peter at the ceiling, as if he was talking to the house, the nursery. 'Don't let Father kill everything.' He turned to his father. 'Oh, I hate you!'

'Insults won't get you anywhere.'

'I wish you were dead!'

'We were, for a long while. Now we're going to really start living. Instead of being handled and massaged, we're going to live.'

Wendy was still crying and Peter joined her again. 'Just a

moment, just one moment, just another moment of nursery,' they wailed.

'Oh George,' said the wife, 'it can't hurt.'

'All right – all right, if they'll only just shut up. One minute, mind you, and then off forever.'

'Daddy, Daddy, Daddy!' sang the children, smiling with wet faces.

'And then we're going on a vacation. David McClean is coming back in half an hour to help us move out and get to the airport. I'm going to dress. You turn the nursery on for a minute, Lydia, just a minute, mind you.'

And the three of them went babbling off while he let himself be vacuumed upstairs through the air flue and set about dressing himself. A minute later Lydia appeared.

'I'll be glad when we get away,' she sighed.

'Did you leave them in the nursery?'

'I wanted to dress too. Oh, that horrid Africa. What can they see in it?'

'Well, in five minutes we'll be on our way to Iowa. Lord, how did we ever get in this house? What prompted us to buy a nightmare?'

'Pride, money, foolishness.'

'I think we'd better get downstairs before those kids get engrossed with those damned beasts again.'

Just then they heard the children calling, 'Daddy, Mommy, come quick – quick!'

They went downstairs in the air flue and ran down the hall. The children were nowhere in sight. 'Wendy? Peter!'

They ran into the nursery. The veldland was empty save for the lions waiting, looking at them. 'Peter, Wendy?'

The door slammed.

'Wendy, Peter!'

George Hadley and his wife whirled and ran back to the door.

'Open the door!' cried George Hadley, trying the knob. 'Why, they've locked it from the outside! Peter!' He beat at the door. 'Open up!'

He heard Peter's voice outside, against the door.

'Don't let them switch off the nursery and the house,' he was
saying.

Mr. and Mrs. George Hadley beat at the door. 'Now, don't
be ridiculous, children. It's time to go. Mr. McClean'll be here
in a minute and . . .'

And then they heard the sounds.

The lions on three sides of them, in the yellow veld grass,
padding through the dry straw, rumbling and roaring in their
throats.

The lions.

Mr. Hadley looked at his wife and they turned and looked
back at the beasts edging slowly forward, crouching, tails stiff.

Mr. and Mrs. Hadley screamed.

And suddenly they realized why those other screams had
sounded familiar.

'Well, here I am,' said David McClean in the nursery door-
way. 'Oh, hello.' He stared at the two children seated in the
centre of the open glade eating a little picnic lunch. Beyond
them was the water hole and the yellow veldland; above was
the hot sun. He began to perspire. 'Where are your father and
mother?'

The children looked up and smiled. 'Oh, they'll be here
directly.'

'Good, we must get going.' At a distance Mr. McClean saw
the lions fighting and clawing and then quieting down to feed in
silence under the shady trees.

He squinted at the lions with his hand up to his eyes.

Now the lions were done feeding. They moved to the water
hole to drink.

A shadow flickered over Mr. McClean's hot face. Many
shadows flickered. The vultures were dropping down the
blazing sky.

'A cup of tea?' asked Wendy in the silence.

*The Illustrated Man shifted in his sleep. He turned,
and each time he turned another picture came to*

*view, colouring his back, his arm, his wrist. He flung
a hand over the dry night grass. The fingers uncurled
and there upon his palm another Illustration stirred
to life. He twisted, and on his chest was an empty
space of stars and blackness, deep, deep, and something moving among those stars, something falling in
the blackness, falling while I watched . . .*

KALEIDOSCOPE

The first concussion cut the rocket up the side with a giant can-opener. The men were thrown into space like a dozen wriggling silverfish. They were scattered into a dark sea; and the ship, in a million pieces, went on, a meteor swarm seeking a lost sun.

'Barkley, Barkley, where are you?'

The sound of voices calling like lost children on a cold night.

'Woode, Woode!'

'Captain!

'Hollis, Hollis, this is Stone.'

'Stone, this is Hollis. Where are you?'

'I don't know. How can I? Which way is up? I'm falling. Good God, I'm falling.'

They fell. They fell as pebbles fall down wells. They were scattered as jackstones are scattered from a gigantic throw. And now instead of men there were only voices – all kinds of voices, disembodied and impassioned, in varying degrees of terror and resignation.

'We're going away from each other.'

This was true. Hollis, swinging head over heels, knew this was true. He knew it with a vague acceptance. They were parting to go their separate ways, and nothing could bring them back. They were wearing their sealed-tight space suits with the glass tubes over their pale faces, but they hadn't had time to lock on their force units. With them they could be small lifeboats in space, saving themselves, saving others, collecting together, finding each other until they were an island of men with some plan. But without the force units snapped to their shoulders they were meteors, senseless, each going to a separate and irrevocable fate.

A period of perhaps ten minutes elapsed while the first terror died and a metallic calm took its place. Space began to weave its strange voices in and out, on a great dark loom, crossing, recrossing, making a final pattern.

'Stone to Hollis. How long can we talk by phone?'

'It depends on how fast you're going your way and I'm going mine.'

'An hour, I make it.'

'That should do it,' said Hollis, abstracted and quiet.

'What happened?' said Hollis a minute later.

'The rocket blew up, that's all. Rockets do blow up.'

'Which way are you going?'

'It looks like I'll hit the moon.'

'It's Earth for me. Back to old Mother Earth at ten thousand miles per hour. I'll burn like a match.' Hollis thought of it with a queer abstraction of mind. He seemed to be removed from his body, watching it fall down and down through space, as objective as he had been in regard to the first falling snowflakes of a winter season long gone.

The others were silent, thinking of the destiny that had brought them to this, falling, falling, and nothing they could do to change it. Even the captain was quiet, for there was no command or plan he knew that could put things back together again.

'Oh, it's a long way down. Oh, it's a long way down, a long, long, long way down,' said a voice. 'I don't want to die, I don't want to die, it's a long way down.'

'Who's that?'

'I don't know.'

'Stimson, I think. Stimson, is that you?'

'It's a long, long way and I don't like it. Oh, God, I don't like it.'

'Stimson, this is Hollis. Stimson, you hear me?'

A pause while they fell separate from one another.

'Stimson?'

'Yes.' He replied at last.

'Stimson, take it easy; we're all in the same fix.'

'I don't want to be here. I want to be somewhere else.'

'There's a chance we'll be found.'

'I must be, I must be,' said Stimson. 'I don't believe this; I don't believe any of this is happening.'

'It's a bad dream,' said someone.

'Shut up!' said Hollis.

'Come and make me,' said the voice. It was Applegate. He laughed easily, with a similar objectivity. 'Come and shut me up.'

Hollis for the first time felt the imposibility of his position. A great anger filled him, for he wanted more than anything at this moment to be able to do something to Applegate. He had wanted for many years to do something and now it was too late. Applegate was only a telephonic voice.

Falling, falling, falling ...

Now, as if they had discovered the horror, two of the men began to scream. In a nightmare Hollis saw one of them float by, very near, screaming and screaming.

'Stop it!' The man was almost at his fingertips, screaming insanely. He would never stop. He would go on screaming for a million miles, as long as he was in radio range, disturbing all of them, making it impossible for them to talk to one another.

Hollis reached out. It was best this way. He made the extra effort and touched the man. He grasped the man's ankle and pulled himself up along the body until he reached the head. The man screamed and clawed frantically, like a drowning swimmer. The screaming filled the universe.

One way or the other, thought Hollis. The moon or Earth or meteors will kill him, so why not now?

He smashed the man's glass mask with his iron fist. The screaming stopped. He pushed off from the body and let it spin away on its own course, falling.

Falling, falling down space Hollis and the rest of them went in the long, endless dropping and whirling of silence.

'Hollis you still there?'

Hollis did not speak, but felt the rush of heat in his face.

'This is Applegate again.'

'All right. Applegate.'

'Let's talk. We haven't anything else to do.'

The captain cut in. 'That's enough of that. We've got to figure a way out of this.'

'Captain, why don't you shut up?' said Applegate.

'What!'

'You heard me, Captain. Don't pull your rank on me, you're ten thousand miles away by now, and let's not kid ourselves. As Stimson puts it, it's a long way down.'

'See here, Applegate!'

'Can it. This is a mutiny of one. I haven't a damn thing to lose. Your ship was a bad ship and you were a bad captain and I hope you break when you hit the Moon.'

'I'm ordering you to stop!'

'Go on, order me again.' Applegate smiled across ten thousand miles. The captain was silent. Applegate continued, 'Where were we, Hollis? Oh yes, I remember. I hate you too. But you know that. You've known it for a long time.'

Hollis clenched his fists, helplessly.

'I want to tell you something,' said Applegate. 'Make you happy. I was the one who blackballed you with the Rocket Company five years ago.'

A meteor flashed by. Hollis looked down and his left hand was gone. Blood spurted. Suddenly there was no air in his suit. He had enough air in his lungs to move his right hand over and twist a knob at his left elbow, tightening the joint and sealing the leak. It had happened so quickly that he was not surprised. Nothing surprised him any more. The air in the suit came back to normal in an instant now that the leak was sealed. And the blood that had flowed so swiftly was pressured as he fastened the knob yet tighter, until it made a tourniquet.

All of this took place in a terrible silence on his part. And the other men chatted. That one man, Lespere, went on and on with his talk about his wife on Mars, his wife on Venus, his wife on Jupiter, his money, his wondrous times, his drunkenness, his gambling, his happiness. On and on, while they all fell. Lespere reminisced on the past, happy, while he fell to his death.

It was so very odd. Space, thousands of miles of space, and these voices vibrating in the centre of it. No one visible at all, and only the radio waves quivering and trying to quicken other men into emotion.

'Are you angry, Hollis?'

'No.' And he was not. The abstraction had returned and he was a thing of dull concrete, forever falling nowhere.

'You wanted to get to the top all your life, Hollis. You always wondered what happened. I put the black mark on you just before I was tossed out myself.'

'That isn't important,' said Hollis. And it was not. It was gone. When life is over it is like a flicker of bright film, an instant on the screen, all of its prejudices and passions condensed and illumined for an instant on space, and before you could cry out, 'There was a happy day, there a bad one, there an evil face, there a good one,' the film burned to a cinder, the screen went dark.

From this outer edge of his life, looking back, there was only one remorse, and that was only that he wished to go on living. Did all dying people feel this way, as if they had never lived? Did life seem that short, indeed, over and done before you took a breath? Did it seem this abrupt and impossible to everyone, or only to himself, here, now, with a few hours left to him for thought and deliberation?

One of the other men, Lespere, was talking. 'Well, I had me a good time: I had a wife on Mars, Venus, and Jupiter. Each of them had money and treated me swell. I got drunk and once I gambled away twenty thousand dollars.'

But you're here now, thought Hollis. I didn't have any of those things. When I was living I was jealous of you, Lespere; when I had another day ahead of me I envied you your women and your good times. Women frightened me and I went into space, always wanting them and jealous of you for having them, and money, and as much happiness as you could have in your own wild way. But now, falling here, with everything over, I'm not jealous of you any more, because it's over for you as it is for me, and right now it's like it never was. Hollis craned his face forward and shouted into the telephone.

'It's all over, Lespere!'

Silence.

'It's just as if it never was, Lespere!'

'Who's that?' Lespere's faltering voice.

'This is Hollis.'

He was being mean. He felt the meanness, the senseless meanness of dying. Applegate had hurt him; now he wanted to hurt another. Applegate and space had both wounded him.

'You're out here, Lespere. It's all over. It's just as if it had never happened, isn't it?'

'No.'

'When anything's over, it's just like it never happened. Where's your life any better than mine, now? Now is what counts. Is it any better? Is it?'

'Yes, it's better!'

'How!'

'Because I got my thoughts, I remember!' cried Lespere, far away, indignant, holding his memories to his chest with both hands.

And he was right. With a feeling of cold water rushing through his head and body, Hollis knew he was right. There were differences between memories and dreams. He had only dreams of things he had wanted to do, while Lespere had memories of things done and accomplished. And this knowledge began to pull Hollis apart, with a slow, quivering precision.

'What good does it do you?' he cried to Lespere. 'Now? When a thing's over it's not good any more. You're no better off than me.'

'I'm resting easy,' said Lespere. 'I've had my turn. I'm not getting mean at the end, like you.'

'Mean?' Hollis turned the word on his tongue. He had never been mean, as long as he could remember, in his life. He had never dared to be mean. He must have saved it all of these years for such a time as this. 'Mean.' He rolled the word into the back of his mind. He felt tears start into his eyes and roll down his face. Someone must have heard his gasping voice.

'Take it easy, Hollis.'

It was, of course, ridiculous. Only a minute before he had been giving advice to others, to Stimson; he had felt a braveness which he had thought to be the genuine thing, and now he knew that it had been nothing but shock and the objectivity possible in shock. Now he was trying to pack a lifetime of suppressed emotion into an interval of minutes.

'I know how you feel, Hollis,' said Lespere, now twenty thousand miles away, his voice fading. 'I don't take it personally.'

But aren't we equal? he wondered. Lespere and I? Here, now? If a thing's over, it's done, and what good is it? You die anyway. But he knew he was rationalizing, for it was like trying to tell the difference between a live man and a corpse. There was a spark in one, and not in the other – an aura, a mysterious element.

So it was with Lespere and himself; Lespere had lived a good full life, and it made him a different man now, and he, Hollis, had been as good as dead for many years. They came to death by separate paths and, in all likelihood, if there were kinds of death, their kinds would be as different as night from day. The quality of death, like that of life, must be of an infinite variety, and if one has already died once, then what was there to look for in dying for good and all, as he was now?

It was a second later that he discovered his right foot was cut sheer away. It almost made him laugh. The air was gone from his suit again. He bent quickly, and there was blood, and the meteor had taken flesh and suit away to the ankle. Oh, death in space was most humorous. It cut you away, piece by piece, like a black and invisible butcher. He tightened the valve at the knee, his head whirling into pain, fighting to remain aware, and with the valve tightened, the blood retained, the air kept, he straightened up and went on falling, falling, for that was all there was left to do.

'Hollis?'

Hollis nodded sleepily, tired of waiting for death.

'This is Applegate again,' said the voice.

'Yes.'

'I've had time to think. I listened to you. This isn't good. It makes us bad. This is a bad way to die. It brings all the bile out. You listening, Hollis?'

'Yes.'

'I lied. A minute ago. I lied. I didn't blackball you. I don't know why I said that. Guess I wanted to hurt you. You seemed the one to hurt. We've always fought. Guess I'm getting old fast and repenting fast. I guess listening to you be mean made me ashamed. Whatever the reason, I want you to know I was an idiot too. There's not an ounce of truth in what I said. To hell with you.'

Hollis felt his heart begin to work again. It seemed as if it hadn't worked for five minutes, but now all of his limbs began to take colour and warmth. The shock was over, and the successive shocks of anger and terror and loneliness were passing. He felt like a man emerging from a cold shower in the morning, ready for breakfast and a new day.

'Thanks, Applegate.'

'Don't mention it. Up your nose, you bastard.'

'Hey,' said Stone.

'What?' Hollis called across space; for Stone, of all of them, was a good friend.

'I've got myself into a metor swarm, some little asteroids.'

'Meteors?'

'I think it's the Myrmidone cluster that goes out past Mars and in toward Earth once every five years. I'm right in the middle. It's like a big kaleidoscope. You get all kinds of colours and shapes and sizes. God, it's beautiful, all that metal.'

Silence.

'I'm going with them,' said Stone. 'They're taking me off with them. I'll be damned.' He laughed.

Hollis looked to see, but saw nothing. There were only the great diamonds and sapphires and emerald mists and velvet inks of space, with God's voice mingling among the crystal fires. There was a kind of wonder and imagination in the thought of Stone going off in the meteor swarm, out past Mars for years and coming in toward Earth every five years, passing in and out of the planet's ken for the next million centuries, Stone and the Myrmidone cluster eternal and unending, shifting and shaping like the kaleidoscope colours when you were a child and held the long tube to the sun and gave it a twirl.

'So long, Hollis.' Stone's voice, very faint now. 'So long.'

'Good luck,' shouted Hollis across thirty thousand miles.

'Don't be funny,' said Stone, and was gone.

The stars closed in.

Now all the voices were fading, each on his own trajectory, some to Mars, others into farthest space. And Hollis himself . . . He looked down. He, of all the others, was going back to Earth alone.

'So long.'

'Take it easy.'

'So long, Hollis.' That was Applegate.

The many good-byes. The short farewells. And now the great loose brain was disintegrating. The components of the brain which had worked so beautifully and efficiently in the skull case of the rocket ship firing through space were dying one by one; the meaning of their life together was falling apart. And as a body dies when the brain ceases functioning, so the spirit of the ship and their long time together and what they meant to one another was dying. Applegate was now no more than a finger blown from the parent body, no longer to be despised and worked against. The brain was exploded, and the senseless, useless fragments of it were far scattered. The voices faded and now all of space was silent. Hollis was alone, falling.

They were all alone. Their voices had died like echoes of the words of God spoken and vibrating in the starred deep. There went the captain to the Moon; there Stone with the meteor swarm; there Stimson; there Applegate toward Pluto; there Smith and Turner and Underwood and all the rest, the shards of the kaleidoscope that had formed a thinking pattern for so long, hurled apart.

And I? thought Hollis. What can I do? Is there anything I can do now to make up for a terrible and empty life? If only I could do one good thing to make up for the meanness I collected all these years and didn't even know was in me! But there's no one here but myself, and how can you do good all alone? You can't. Tomorrow night I'll hit Earth's atmosphere.

I'll burn, he thought, and be scattered in ashes all over the continental lands. I'll be put to use. Just a little bit, but ashes are ashes and they'll add to the land.

He fell swiftly, like a bullet, like a pebble, like an iron weight, objective, objective all of the time now, not sad or happy or anything, but only wishing he could do a good thing now that everything was gone, a good thing for just himself to know about.

When I hit the atmosphere, I'll burn like a meteor.

'I wonder,' he said, 'if anyone'll see me?'

The small boy on the country road looked up and screamed. 'Look, Mom, look! A falling star!'

The blazing white star fell down the sky of dusk in Illinois.

'Make a wish,' said his mother. 'Make a wish.'

The Illustrated Man turned in the moonlight. He turned again . . . and again . . . and again. . . .

THE OTHER FOOT

When they heard the news they came out of the restaurants and cafés and hotels and looked at the sky. They lifted their dark hands over their upturned white eyes. Their mouths hung wide. In the hot noon for thousands of miles there were little towns where the dark people stood with their shadows under them, looking up.

In her kitchen Hattie Johnson covered the boiling soup, wiped her thin fingers on a cloth, and walked carefully to the back porch.

'Come on, Ma! Hey, Ma, come on – you'll miss it!'

'Hey, Mom!'

Three little Negro boys danced around in the dusty yard, yelling. Now and then they looked at the house frantically.

'I'm coming,' said Hattie, and opened the screen door. 'Where you hear this rumour?'

'Up at Jones's, Ma. They say a rocket's coming, first one in twenty years, with a white man in it!'

'What's a white man? I never seen one.'

'You'll find out,' said Hattie. 'Yes indeed, you'll find out.'

'Tell us about one, Ma. Tell like you did.'

Hattie frowned. 'Well, it's been a long time. I was a little girl, you see. That was back in 1965.'

'Tell us about a white man, Mom!'

She came and stood in the yard, looking up at the blue clear Martian sky with the thin white Martian clouds, and in the distance the Martian hills broiling in the heat. She said at last, 'Well, first of all, they got white hands.'

'White hands!' The boys joked, slapping each other.

'And they got white arms.'

'White arms!' hooted the boys.

'And white faces.'

'White faces! *Really?*'

'White like *this*, Mom?' The smallest threw dust on his face, sneezing. 'This way?'

'Whiter than that,' she said gravely, and turned to the sky again. There was a troubled thing in her eyes, as if she was looking for a thundershower up high, and not seeing it made her worry. 'Maybe you better go inside.'

'Oh, Mom!' They stared at her in disbelief. 'We got to watch, we just got to. Nothing's going to happen, is it?'

'I don't know. I got a feeling, is all.'

'We just want to see the ship and maybe run down to the port and see that white man. What's he like, huh, Mom?'

'I don't know. I just don't know,' she mused, shaking her head.

'Tell us some more!'

'Well, the white people live on Earth, which is where we all come from, twenty years ago. We just up and walked away and came to Mars and set down and built towns and here we are. Now, we're Martians instead of Earth people. And no white men've come up here in all that time. That's the story.'

'Why didn't they come up, Mom?'

'Well, 'cause. Right after we got up here, Earth got in an atom war. They blew each other up terribly. They forgot us. When they finished fighting, after years, they didn't have any rockets. Took them until recently to build more. So here they come now, twenty years later, to visit.' She gazed at her children numbly and then began to walk. 'You wait here. I'm going down the line to Elizabeth Brown's house. You promise to stay?'

'We don't want to but we will.'

'All right, then.' And she ran off down the road.

At the Browns' she arrived in time to see everybody packed into the family car. 'Hey there, Hattie! Come on along!'

'Where you going?' she said, breathlessly running up.

'To see the white man!'

'That's right,' said Mr. Brown seriously. He waved at his load. 'These children never saw one, and *I* almost forgot.'

'What you going to do with that white man?' asked Hattie.

'Do?' said everyone. 'Why – just *look* at him, is all.'

'You sure?'

'What else *can* we do?'

'I don't know,' said Hattie. 'I just thought there might be trouble.'

'What kind of trouble,'

'You *know*,' said Hattie vaguely, embarrassed. 'You ain't going to lynch him?'

'Lynch him?' Everyone laughed. Mr. Brown slapped his knee. 'Why, bless you, child, no! We're going to shake his hand. Ain't we, everyone?'

'Sure, sure!'

Another car drove up from another direction and Hattie gave a cry. 'Willie!'

'What you doing 'way down here? Where're the kids?' shouted her husband angrily. He glared at the others. 'You going down like a bunch of fools to see that man come in?'

'That appears to be just right,' agreed Mr. Brown, nodding and smiling.

'Well, take your guns along,' said Willie. 'I'm on my way home for mine right now!'

'Willie!'

'You get in this car, Hattie.' He held the door open firmly, looking at her until she obeyed. Without another word to the others he roared the car down the dusty road.

'Willie, not so fast!'

'Not so fast, huh? We'll see about that.' He watched the road tear under the car. 'What right they got coming up here this late? Why don't they leave us in peace? Why didn't they blow themselves up on that old world and let us be?'

'Willie, that ain't no Christian way to talk.'

'I'm not feeling Christian,' he said savagely, gripping the wheel. 'I'm just feeling mean. After all them years of doing what they did to our folks – my mom and dad, and your mom and dad— You remember? You remember how they hung my father on Knockwood Hill and shot my mother? You remember? Or you got a memory that's short like the others?'

'I remember,' she said.

'You remember Dr. Phillips and Mr. Burton and their big houses, and my mother's washing shack, and Dad working when he was old, and the thanks he got was being hung by Dr. Phillips and Mr. Burton. Well,' said Willie, 'the shoe's on the other foot now. We'll see who gets laws passed against him, who gets lynched, who rides the back of streetcars, who gets segregated in shows. We'll just wait and see.'

'Oh, Willie, you're talking trouble.'

'Everybody's talking. Everybody's thought on this day, thinking it'd never be. Thinking. What kind of day would it be if the white man ever came up here to Mars? But here's the day, and we can't run away.'

'Ain't you going to let the white people live up here?'

'Sure.' He smiled, but it was a wide, mean smile, and his eyes were mad. 'They can come up and live and work here, why, certainly. All they got to do to deserve it is live in their own small part of town, the slums, and shine our shoes for us, and mop up our trash, and sit in the last row in the balcony. That's all we ask. And once a week we hang one or two of them. Simple.'

'You don't sound human, and I don't like it.'

'You'll have to get used to it,' he said. He braked the car to a stop before the house and jumped out. 'Find my guns and some rope. We'll do this right.'

'Oh, Willie,' she wailed, and just sat there in the car while he ran up the steps and slammed the front door.

She went along. She didn't want to go along, but he rattled around in the attic, cursing like a crazy man until he found four guns. She saw the brutal metal of them glittering in the black attic, and she couldn't see him at all, he was so dark; she heard only his swearing, and at last his long legs came climbing down from the attic in a shower of dust, and he stacked up bunches of brass shells and blew out the gun chambers and clicked shells into them, his face stern and heavy and folded in upon the gnawing bitterness there. 'Leave us alone,' he kept muttering, his hands flying away from him suddenly, uncontrolled. 'Leave us blame alone, why don't they?'

'Willie, Willie.'

'You too – you too.' And he gave her the same look, and a pressure of his hatred touched her mind.

Outside the window the boys gabbled to each other. 'White as milk, she said. White as milk.'

'White as a stone, like chalk you write with.'

Willie plunged out of the house. 'You children come inside, I'm locking you up. You ain't seeing no white man, you ain't talking about them, you ain't doing nothing. Come on now.'

'But, Daddy—'

He shoved them through the door and went· fetched a bucket of paint and a stencil and from the garage a long thick hairy rope coil into which he fashioned a hangman's knot, very carefully, watching the sky while his hands felt their way at their task.

And then they were in the car, leaving bolls of dust behind them down the road. 'Slow up, Willie.'

'This is no slowing-up time,' he said. 'This is a hurrying time, and I'm hurrying.'

All along the road people were looking up in the sky, or climbing in their cars, or riding in cars, and guns were sticking up out of some cars like telescopes sighting all the evils of a world coming to an end.

She looked at the guns. 'You been talking,' she accused her husband.

'That's what I been doing,' he grunted, nodding. He watched the road, fiercely. 'I stopped at every house and I told them what to do, to get their guns, to get paint, to bring rope and be ready. And here we all are, the welcoming committee, to give them the key to the city. Yes, sir!'

She pressed her thin dark hands together to push away the terror growing in her now, and she felt the car bucket and lurch around other cars. She heard the voices yelling, Hey, Willie, look! and hands holding up ropes and guns as they rushed by! and mouths smiling at them in the swift rushing.

'Here we are,' said Willie, and braked the car into dusty halting and silence. He kicked the door open with a big foot and, laden with weapons, stepped out, lugging them across the airport meadow.

'Have you *thought*, Willie?'

'That's all I done for twenty years. I was sixteen when I left Earth, and I was glad to leave,' he said. 'There wasn't anything there for me or you or anybody like us. I've never been sorry I left. We've had peace here, the first time we ever drew a solid breath. Now, come on.'

He pushed through the dark crowd which came to meet him.

'Willie, Willie, what we gonna do?' they said.

'Here's a gun,' he said. 'Here's a gun. Here's another.' He passed them out with savage jabs of his arms. 'Here's a pistol. Here's a shotgun.'

The people were so close together it looked like one dark body with a thousand arms reaching out to take the weapons. 'Willie, Willie.'

His wife stood tall and silent by him, her fluted lips pressed shut, and her large eyes wet and tragic. 'Bring the paint,' he said to her. And she lugged a gallon can of yellow paint across the field to where, at that moment, a trolley car was pulling up, with a fresh-painted sign on its front, TO THE WHITE MAN'S LANDING, full of talking people who got off and ran across the meadow, stumbling, looking up. Women with picnic boxes, men with straw hats, in shirt sleeves. The streetcar stood humming and empty. Willie climbed up, set the paint cans down, opened them, stirred the paint, rested a brush, drew forth a stencil, and climbed up on a seat.

'Hey, there!' The conductor came around behind him, his coin changer jangling. 'What you think you're doing? Get down off there!'

'You see what I'm doing. Keep your shirt on.'

And Willie began the stencilling in yellow paint. He dabbed on an *F* and an *O* and an *R* with terrible pride in his work. And when he finished it the conductor squinted up and read the fresh glinting yellow words, FOR WHITES: REAR SECTION. He read it again. FOR WHITES. He blinked. REAR SECTION. The conductor looked at Willie and began to smile.

'Does that suit you?' asked Willie, stepping down.

Said the conductor, 'That suits me just fine, sir.'

Hattie was looking at the sign from outside, and holding her hands over her breasts.

Willie returned to the crowd, which was growing now, taking size from every auto that groaned to a halt, and every new trolley car which squealed around the bend from the nearby town.

Willie climbed up on a packing box. 'Let's have a delegation to paint every streetcar in the next hour. Volunteers?'

Hands leapt up.

'Get going!'

They went.

'Let's have a delegation to fix theatre seats, roped off, the last two rows for whites.'

More hands.

'Go on!'

They ran off.

Willie peered around, bubbled with perspiration, panting with exertion, proud of his energy, his hand on his wife's shoulder who stood under him looking at the ground with her downcast eyes. 'Let's see now,' he declared. 'Oh yes. We got to pass a law this afternoon; no intermarriages!'

'That's right,' said a lot of people.

'All shoeshine boys quit their jobs today.'

'Quittin' right now!' Some men threw down the rags they carried, in their excitement, all across town.

'Got to pass a minimum wage law, don't we?'

'Sure!'

'Pay them white folks at least ten cents an hour.'

'That's right!'

The mayor of the town hurried up. 'Now look here, Willie Johnson. Get down off that box!'

'Mayor, I can't be made to do nothing like that.'

'You're making a mob, Willie Johnson.'

'That's the idea.'

'The same thing you always hated when you were a kid. You're no better than some of those white men you yell about!'

'This is the other shoe, Mayor, and the other foot,' said Willie, not even looking at the mayor, looking at the faces beneath him, some of them smiling, some of them doubtful, others bewildered, some of them reluctant and drawing away, fearful.

'You'll be sorry,' said the mayor.

'We'll have an election and get a new mayor,' said Willie. And he glanced off at the town where up and down the streets signs were being hung, fresh-painted: LIMITED CLIENTELE: *Right to serve customer revocable at any time.* He grinned and slapped his hands. Lord! And streetcars were being halted and sections being painted white in back, to suggest their future inhabitants. And theatres were being invaded and roped off by chuckling men, while their wives stood wondering on the curbs and children were spanked into houses to be hid away from this awful time.

'Are we all ready?' called Willie Johnson, the rope in his hands with the noose tied and neat.

'Ready!' shouted half the crowd. The other half murmured and moved like figures in a nightmare in which they wished no participation.

'Here it comes!' called a small boy.

Like marionette heads on a single string, the heads of the crowd turned upward.

Across the sky, very high and beautiful, a rocket burned on a sweep of orange fire. It circled and came down, causing all to gasp. It landed, setting the meadow afire here and there; the fire burned out, the rocket lay a moment in quiet, and then, as the silent crowd watched, a great door in the side of the vessel whispered out a breath of oxygen, the door slid back and an old man stepped out.

'A white man, a white man, a white man ...' The words travelled back in the expectant crowd, the children speaking in each other's ears, whispering, butting each other, the words moving in ripples to where the crowd stopped and the street-cars stood in the windy sunlight, the smell of paint coming out of their opened windows. The whispering wore itself away and it was gone.

No one moved.

The white man was tall and straight, but a deep weariness

was in his face. He had not shaved this day, and his eyes were as old as the eyes of a man can be and still be alive. His eyes were colourless; almost white and sightless with things he had seen in the passing years. He was as thin as a winter bush. His hands trembled and he had to lean against the portway of the ship as he looked out over the crowd.

He put out a hand and half smiled, but drew his hand back. No one moved.

He looked down into their faces, and perhaps he saw but did not see the guns and the ropes, and perhaps he smelled the paint. No one ever asked him. He began to talk. He started very quietly and slowly, expecting no interruptions, and receiving none, and his voice was very tired and old and pale.

'It doesn't matter who I am,' he said. 'I'd be just a name to you, anyhow. I don't know your names, either. That'll come later.' He paused, closed his eyes for a moment, and then continued:

'Twenty years ago you left Earth. That's a long, long time. It's more like twenty centuries, so much has happened. After you left, the War came.' He nodded slowly. 'Yes, the *big* one. The Third One. It went on for a long time. Until last year. We bombed all of the cities of the world. We destroyed New York and London and Moscow and Paris and Shanghai and Bombay and Alexandria. We ruined it all. And when we finished with the big cities we went to the little cities and atom-bombed and burned them.'

Now he began to name cities and places, and streets. And as he named them, a murmur rose up in his audience.

'We destroyed Natchez ...'

A murmur.

'And Columbus, Georgia ...'

Another murmur.

'We burned New Orleans ...'

A sigh.

'And Atlanta ...'

Still another.

'And there was nothing left of Greenwater, Alabama.'

Willie Johnson jerked his head and his mouth opened. Hattie

saw this gesture, and the recognition coming into his dark eyes.

'Nothing was left,' said the old man in the port, speaking slowly. 'Cotton fields, burned.'

Oh, said everyone.

'Cotton mills bombed out—'

'Oh.'

'And the factories, radioactive; everything radioactive. All the roads and the farms and the foods, radioactive. Everything.' He named more names of towns and villages.

'Tampa.'

'That's my town,' someone whispered.

'Fulton.'

'That's mine,' someone else said.

'Memphis.'

'Memphis. Did they burn *Memphis*?' A shocked query.

'Memphis, blown up.'

'*Fourth* Street in Memphis?'

'All of it,' said the old man.

It was stirring them now. After twenty years it was rushing back. The towns and the places, the trees and the brick buildings, the signs and the churches and the familiar stores, all of it was coming to the surface among the gathered people. Each name touched memory, and there was no one present without a thought of another day. They were all old enough for that, save the children.

'Laredo.'

'I remember Laredo.'

'New York City.'

'I had a store in Harlem.'

'Harlem, bombed out.'

The ominous words. The familiar, remembered places. The struggle to imagine all of those places in ruins.

Willie Johnson murmured the words, 'Greenwater, Alabama. That's where I was born, I remember.'

Gone. All of it gone. The man said so.

The man continued, 'So we destroyed everything and ruined everything, like the fools that we were and the fools that we are. We killed millions. I don't think there are more than five hundred thousand people left in the world, all kinds and types. And out of all the wreckage we salvaged enough metal to build this rocket, and we came to Mars in it this month to seek your help.'

He hesitated and looked down among the faces to see what could be found there, but he was uncertain.

Hattie Johnson felt her husband's arm tense, saw his fingers grip the rope.

'We've been fools,' said the old man quietly. 'We've brought the Earth and civilization down about our heads. None of the cities are worth saving – they'll be radioactive for a century. Earth is over and done with. Its age is through. You have rockets here which you haven't tried to use to return to Earth in twenty years. Now I've come to ask you to use them. To come to Earth, to pick up the survivors and bring them back to Mars. To help us go on at this time. We've been stupid. Before God we admit our stupidity and our evilness. All the Chinese and the Indians and the Russians and the British and the Americans. We're asking to be taken in. Your Martian soil has lain fallow for numberless centuries; there's room for everyone; it's good soil – I've seen your fields from above. We'll come and work it *for* you. Yes, we'll even do that. We deserve anything you want to do to us, but don't shut us out. We can't force you to act now. If you want I'll get into my ship and go back and that will be all there is to it. We won't bother you again. But we'll come here and we'll work for you—and do the things you did for us – clean your houses, cook your meals, shine your shoes, and humble ourselves in the sight of God for the things we have done over the centuries to ourselves, to others, to you.'

He was finished.

There was a silence of silences. A silence you could hold in your hand and a silence that came down like a pressure of a distant storm over the crowd. Their long arms hung like dark pendulums in the sunlight, and their eyes were upon the old man and he did not move now, but waited.

Willie Johnson held the rope in his hands. Those around him

watched to see what he might do. His wife Hattie waited, clutching his arm.

She wanted to get at the hate of them all, to pry at it and work at it until she found a little chink, and then pull out a pebble or a stone or a brick and then a part of the wall, and, once started, the whole edifice might roar down and be done away with. It was teetering now. But which was the keystone, and how to get at it? How to touch them and get a thing started in all of them to make a ruin of their hate?

She looked at Willie there in the strong silence and the only thing she knew about the situation was him and his life and what had happened to him, and suddenly he was the keystone; suddenly she knew that if he could be pried loose, then the thing in all of them might be loosened and torn away.

'Mister—' She stepped forward. She didn't even know the first words to say. The crowd stared at her back; she felt them staring. 'Mister—'

The man turned to her with a tired smile.

'Mister,' she said, 'do you know Knockwood Hill in Greenwater, Alabama?'

The old man spoke over his shoulder to someone within the ship. A moment later a photographic map was handed out and the man held it, waiting.

'You know the big oak on top of that hill, mister?'

The big oak. The place where Willie's father was shot and hung and found swinging in the morning wind.

'Yes.'

'Is that still there?' asked Hattie.

'It's gone,' said the old man. 'Blown up. The hill's all gone, and the oak tree too. You see?' He touched the photograph.

'Let me see that,' said Willie, jerking forward and looking at the map.

Hattie blinked at the white man, heart pounding.

'Tell me about Greenwater,' she said quickly.

'What do you want to know?'

'About Dr. Phillips. Is he still alive?'

A moment in which the information was found in a clicking machine within the rocket . . .

'Killed in the war.'

'And his son?'

'Dead.'

'What about their house?'

'Burned. Like all the other houses.'

'What about that other big tree on Knockwood Hill?'

'All the trees went – burned.'

'*That* tree went, you're sure?' said Willie.

'Yes.'

Willie's body loosened somewhat.

'And what about that Mr. Burton's house and Mr. Burton?'

'No houses at all left, no people.'

'You know Mrs. Johnson's washing shack, my mother's place?'

The place where she was shot.

'That's gone too. Everything's gone. Here are the pictures, you can see for yourself.'

The pictures were there to be held and looked at and thought about. The rocket was full of pictures and answers to questions. Any town, any building, any place.

Willie stood with the rope in his hands.

He was remembering Earth, the green Earth and the green town where he was born and raised, and he was thinking now of that town, gone to pieces, to ruin, blown up and scattered, all of the landmarks with it, all of the supposed or certain evil scattered with it, all of the hard men gone, the stables, the ironsmiths, the curio shops, the soda founts, the gin mills, the river bridges, the lynching trees, the buckshot-covered hills, the roads, the cows, the mimosas, and his own house as well as those big-pillared houses down near the long river, those white mortuaries where the women as delicate as moths fluttered in the autumn light, distant, far away. Those houses where the cold men rocked, with glasses of drink in their hands, guns leaned against the porch newels, sniffing the autumn airs and considering death. Gone, all gone; gone and never coming back. Now, for certain, all of that civilization ripped into confetti and strewn at their feet. Nothing, nothing of it left to hate – not an empty brass gun shell, or a twisted hemp, or a tree, or even a hill of it to hate. Nothing but some alien people in a rocket, people who might shine his shoes and ride in the back of trolleys or sit far up in midnight theatres . . .

'You won't have to do that,' said Willie Johnson.

His wife glanced at his big hands.

His fingers were opening.

The rope, released, fell and coiled upon itself along the ground.

They ran through the streets of their town and tore down the new signs so quickly made, and painted out the fresh yellow signs on streetcars, and they cut down the ropes in the theatre balconies, and unloaded their guns and stacked their ropes away.

'A new start for everyone,' said Hattie, on the way home in their car.

'Yes,' said Willie at last. 'The Lord's let us come through, a few here and a few there. And what happens next is up to all of us. The time for being fools is over. We got to be something else except fools. I knew that when he talked. I knew then that now the white man's as lonely as we've always been. He's got no home now, just like we didn't have one for so long. Now everything's even. We can start all over again, on the same level.'

He stopped the car and sat in it, not moving, while Hattie went to let the children out. They ran down to see their father. 'You see the white man? You see him?' they cried.

'Yes, sir,' said Willie, sitting behind the wheel, rubbing his face with his slow fingers. 'Seems like for the first time today I really seen the white man – I really seen him clear.'

THE HIGHWAY

The cooling afternoon rain had come over the valley, touching the corn in the tilled mountain fields, tapping on the dry grass roof of the hut. In the rainy darkness the woman ground corn between cakes of lava rock, working steadily. In the wet light-lessness, somewhere, a baby cried.

Hernando stood waiting for the rain to cease so he might take the wooden plough into the field again. Below, the river boiled brown and thickened in its course. The concrete highway, another river, did not flow at all; it lay shining, empty. A car had not come along it in an hour. This was, in itself, of unusual interest. Over the years there had not been an hour when a car had not pulled up, someone shouting, 'Hey there, can we take your picture?' Someone with a box that clicked, and a coin in his hand. If he walked slowly across the field without his hat, sometimes they called, 'Oh, we want you with your hat on!' And they waved their hands, rich with gold things that told time, or identified them, or did nothing at all but winked like spider's eyes in the sun. So he would turn and go back to get his hat.

His wife spoke. 'Something is wrong, Hernando?'

'Si. The road. Something big has happened. Something big to make the road so empty this way.'

He walked from the hut slowly and easily, the rain washing over the twined shoes of grass and thick tyre rubber he wore. He remembered very well the incident of this pair of shoes. The tyre had come into the hut with violence one night, ex-ploding the chickens and the pots apart! It had come alone, rolling swiftly. The car, off which it had come, had rushed on, as far as the curve, and hung a moment, headlights reflected, before plunging into the river. The car was still there. One might see it on a good day, when the river ran slow and the mud cleared. Deep under, shining its metal, long and low and very rich, lay the car. But then the mud came in again and you saw nothing.

The following day he had carved the shoe soles from the tyre rubber.

He reached the highway now, and stood upon it, listening to the small sounds it made in the rain.

Then, suddenly, as if at a signal, the cars came. Hundreds of them, miles of them, rushing and rushing as he stood, by and by him. The big long black cars heading north toward the United States, roaring, taking the curves at too great a speed. With a ceaseless blowing and honking. And there was something about the faces of the people packed into the cars, something which dropped him into a deep silence. He stood back to let the cars roar on. He counted them until he tired. Five hundred, a thousand cars passed, and there was something in the faces of all of them. But they moved too swiftly for him to tell what this thing was.

Finally the silence and emptiness returned. The swift long low convertible cars were gone. He heard the last horn fade.

The road was empty again.

It had been like a funeral cortège. But a wild one, racing, hair out, screaming to some ceremony ever northward. Why? He could only shake his head and rub his fingers softly, at his sides.

Now, all alone, a final car. There was something very, very final about it. Down the mountain road in the thin cool rain, fuming up great clouds of steam, came an old Ford. It was travelling as swiftly as it might. He expected it to break apart any instant. When this ancient Ford saw Hernando it pulled up, caked with mud and rusted, the radiator bubbling angrily.

'May we have some water, please, señor!'

A young man, perhaps twenty-one, was driving. He wore a yellow sweater, an open-collared white shirt and grey pants. In the topless car the rain fell upon him and five young women packed so they could not move in the interior. They were all very pretty and they were keeping the rain from themselves and the driver with old newspapers. But the rain got through to them, soaking their bright dresses, soaking the young man. His hair was plastered with rain. But they did not seem to care.

None complained, and this was unusual. Always before they complained; of rain, of heat, of time, of cold, of distance.

Hernando nodded. 'I'll bring you water.'

'Oh, please hurry!' one of the girls cried. She sounded very high and afraid. There was no impatience in her, only an asking out of fear. For the first time Hernando ran when a tourist asked; always before he had walked slower at such requests.

He returned with a hub lid full of water. This, too, had been a gift from the highway. One afternoon it had sailed like a flung coin into his field, round and glittering. The car to which it belonged had slid on, oblivious to the fact that it had lost a silver eye. Until now, he and his wife had used it for washing and cooking; it made a fine bowl.

As he poured the water into the boiling radiator, Hernando looked up at their stricken faces. 'Oh, thank you, thank you,' said one of the girls. 'You don't know what this means.'

Hernando smiled. 'So much traffic in this hour. It all goes one way. North.'

He did not mean to say anything to hurt them. But when he looked up again there all of them sat, in the rain, and they were crying. They were crying very hard. And the young man was trying to stop them by laying his hands on their shoulders and shaking them gently, one at a time, but they held their papers over their heads and their mouths moved and their eyes were shut and their faces changed colour and they cried, some loud, some soft.

Hernando stood with the half-empty lid in his fingers. 'I did not mean to say anything, señor,' he apologized.

'That's all right,' said the driver.

'What is wrong, señor?'

'Haven't you heard?' replied the young man, turning, holding tightly to the wheel with one hand, leaning forward. 'It's happened.'

This was bad. The others, at this, cried still harder, holding on to each other, forgetting the newspapers, letting the rain fall and mingle with their tears.

Hernando stiffened. He put the rest of the water into the radiator. He looked at the sky, which was black with storm. He looked at the river rushing. He felt the asphalt under his shoes.

He came to the side of the car. The young man took his hand and gave him a peso. 'No.' Hernando gave it back. 'It is my pleasure.'

'Thank you, you're so kind,' said one of the girls, still sobbing. 'Oh, Mama, Papa. Oh, I want to be home, I want to be home. Oh, Mama, Dad.' And others held her.

'I did not hear, señor,' said Hernando quietly.

'The war!' shouted the young man as if no one could hear. 'It's come, the atom war, the end of the world!'

'Señor, señor,' said Hernando.

'Thank you, thank you for your help. Good-bye,' said the young man.

'Good-bye,' they all said in the rain, not seeing him.

He stood while the car engaged its gears and rattled off down, fading away, through the valley. Finally it was gone, with the young women in it, the last car, the newspapers held and fluttered over their heads.

Hernando did not move for a long time. The rain ran very cold down his cheeks and along his fingers and into the woven garment on his legs. He held his breath, waiting, tight and tensed.

He watched the highway, but it did not move again. He doubted that it would move much for a very long time.

The rain stopped. The sky broke through the clouds. In ten minutes the storm was gone, like a bad breath. A sweet wind blew the smell of the jungle up to him. He could hear the river moving gently and easily on its way. The jungle was very green; everything was fresh. He walked down through the field to his house and picked up his plough. With his hands on it he looked at the sky beginning to burn hot with the sun.

His wife called out from her work. 'What happened, Hernando?'

'It is nothing,' he replied.

He set the plough in the furrow, he called sharply to his burro, 'Burrrrrrr-o!' And they walked together through the rich field, under the clearing sky, on their tilled land by the deep river.

'What do they mean, "the world"?' he said.

THE MAN

Captain Hart stood in the door of the rocket. 'Why don't they come?' he said.

'Who knows?' said Martin, his lieutenant. 'Do I know, Captain?'

'What kind of a place is this, anyway?' The captain lighted a cigar. He tossed the match out into the glittering meadow. The grass started to burn.

Martin moved to stamp it out with his boot.

'No,' ordered Captain Hart, 'let it burn. Maybe they'll come see what's happening then, the ignorant fools.'

Martin shrugged and withdrew his foot from the spreading fire.

Captain Hart examined his watch. 'An hour ago we landed here, and does the welcoming committee rush out with a brass band to shake out hands? No indeed! Here we ride millions of miles through space and the fine citizens of some silly town on some unknown planet ignore us!' He snorted, tapping his watch. 'Well, I'll just give them five more minutes, and then—'

'And then what?' asked Martin, ever so politely, watching the captain's jowls shake.

'We'll fly over their damned city again and scare hell out of them.' His voice grew quieter. 'Do you think, Martin, maybe they didn't see us land?'

'They saw us. They looked up as we flew over.'

'Then why aren't they running across the field? Are they hiding? Are they yellow?'

Martin shook his head. 'No. Take these binoculars, sir. See for yourself. Everybody's walking around. They're not frightened. They – well, they just don't seem to care.'

Captain Hart placed the binoculars to his tired eyes. Martin looked up and had time to observe the lines and the grooves of irritation, tiredness, nervousness there. Hart looked a million years old; he never slept, he ate little, and drove himself on, on. Now his mouth moved, aged and drear, but sharp, under the held binoculars.

'Really, Martin, I don't know why we bother. We build rockets, we go to all the trouble of crossing space, searching for them, and this is what we get. Neglect. Look at those idiots wandering about in there. Don't they realize how big this is? The first space flight to touch their provincial land. How many times does that happen? Are they that blasé?'

Martin didn't know.

Captain Hart gave him back the binoculars wearily. 'Why do we do it, Martin? This space travel, I mean. Always on the go. Always searching. Our insides always tight, never any rest.'

'Maybe we're looking for peace and quiet. Certainly there's none on Earth,' said Martin.

'No, there's not, is there?' Captain Hart was thoughtful, the fire damped down. 'Not since Darwin, eh? Not since everything went by the board, everything we used to believe in, eh? Divine power and all that. And so you think maybe that's why we're going out to the stars, eh, Martin? Looking for our lost souls, is that it? Trying to get away from our evil planet to a good one?'

'Perhaps, sir. Certainly we're looking for something.'

Captain Hart cleared his throat and tightened back into sharpness. 'Well, right now we're looking for the mayor of that city there. Run in, tell them who we are, the first rocket expedition to Planet Forty-three in Star System Three. Captain Hart sends his salutations and desires to meet the mayor. On the double!'

'Yes, sir.' Martin walked slowly across the meadow.

'Hurry!' snapped the captain.

'Yes, sir!' Martin trotted away. Then he walked again, smiling to himself.

The captain had smoked two cigars before Martin returned.

Martin stopped and looked up into the door of the rocket, swaying, seemingly unable to focus his eyes or think.

'Well?' snapped Hart. 'What happened? Are they coming to welcome us?'

'No.' Martin had to lean dizzily against the ship.

'Why not?'

'It's not important,' said Martin. 'Give me a cigarette, please, Captain.' His fingers groped blindly at the rising pack, for he was looking at the golden city and blinking. He lighted one and smoked quietly for a long time.

'Say something!' cried the captain. 'Aren't they interested in our rocket?'

Martin said, 'What? Oh. The rocket?' He inspected his cigarette. 'No, they're not interested. Seems we came at an inopportune time.'

'Inopportune time!'

Martin was patient. 'Captain, listen. Something big happened yesterday in that city. It's so big, so important, that we're second-rate – second fiddle. I've *got* to sit down.' He lost his balance and sat heavily, gasping for air.

The captain chewed his cigar angrily. 'What happened?'

Martin lifted his head, smoke from the burning cigarette in his fingers, blowing in the wind. 'Sir, yesterday, in that city, a remarkable man appeared – good, intelligent, compassionate, and infinitely wise!'

The captain glared at his lieutenant. 'What's that to do with us?'

'It's hard to explain. But he was a man for whom they'd waited a long time – a million years maybe. And yesterday he walked into their city. That's why today, sir, our rocket landing means nothing.'

The captain sat down violently. 'Who was it? Not Ashley? He didn't arrive in his rocket before us and steal my glory, did he?' He seized Martin's arm. His face was pale and dismayed.

'Not Ashley, sir.'

'Then it was Burton! I knew it. Burton stole in ahead of us and ruined my landing! You can't trust anyone any more.'

'Not Burton either, sir,' said Martin quietly.

The captain was incredulous. 'There were only three rockets.

We were in the lead. This man who got here ahead of us? What was his name!'

'He didn't have a name. He doesn't need one. It would be different on every planet, sir.'

The captain stared at his lieutenant with hard, cynical eyes.

'Well, what did he do that was so wonderful that nobody even looks at our ship?'

'For one thing,' said Martin steadily, 'he healed the sick and comforted the poor. He fought hypocrisy and dirty politics and sat among the people, talking, through the day.'

'Is that so wonderful?'

'Yes, Captain.'

'I don't get this.' The captain confronted Martin, peered into his face and eyes. 'You been drinking, eh?' He was suspicious. He backed away. 'I don't understand.'

Martin looked at the city. 'Captain, if you don't understand, there's no way of telling you.'

The captain followed his gaze. The city was quiet and beautiful and a great peace lay over it. The captain stepped forward, taking his cigar from his lips. He squinted first at Martin, then at the golden spires of the buildings.

'You don't mean – you *can't* mean— That man you're talking about couldn't be—'

Martin nodded. 'That's what I mean, sir.'

The captain stood silently, not moving. He drew himself up.

'I don't believe it,' he said at last.

At high noon Captain Hart walked briskly into the city, accompanied by Lieutenant Martin and an assistant who was carrying some electrical equipment. Every once in a while the captain laughed loudly, put his hands on his hips and shook his head.

The mayor of the town confronted him. Martin set up a tripod, screwed a box on to it, and switched on the batteries.

'Are you the mayor?' The captain jabbed a finger out.

'I am,' said the mayor.

The delicate apparatus stood between them, controlled and adjusted by Martin and the assistant. Instantaneous translations from any language were made by the box. The words sounded crisply on the mild air of the city.

'About this occurrence yesterday,' said the captain. 'It occurred?'

'It did.'

'You have witnesses?'

'We have.'

'May we talk to them?'

'Talk to any of us,' said the mayor. 'We are all witnesses.'

In an aside to Martin the captain said, 'Mass hallucination.' To the mayor, 'What did this man – this stranger – look like?'

'That would be hard to say,' said the mayor, smiling a little.

'Why would it?'

'Opinions might differ slightly.'

'I'd like your opinion, sir, anyway,' said the captain. 'Record this,' he snapped to Martin over his shoulder. The lieutenant pressed the button of a hand recorder.

'Well,' said the mayor of the city, 'he was a very gentle and kind man. He was of a great and knowing intelligence.'

'Yes – yes, I know, I know.' The captain waved his fingers. 'Generalizations. I want something specific. What did he look like?'

'I don't believe that is important,' replied the mayor.

'It's very important,' said the captain sternly. 'I want a description of this fellow. If I can't get it from you, I'll get it from others.' To Martin, 'I'm sure it must have been Burton, pulling one of his practical jokes.'

Martin would not look him in the face. Martin was coldly silent.

The captain snapped his fingers. 'There was something or other – a healing?'

'Many healings,' said the mayor.

'May I see one?'

'You may,' said the mayor. 'My son.' He nodded at a small boy who stepped forward. 'He was afflicted with a withered arm. Now, look upon it.'

At this the captain laughed tolerantly. 'Yes, yes. This isn't even circumstantial evidence, you know. I didn't see the boy's withered arm. I see only his arm whole and well. That's no proof. What proof have you that the boy's arm was withered yesterday and today is well?'

'My word is my proof,' said the mayor simply.

'My dear man!' cried the captain. 'You don't expect me to go on hearsay, do you? Oh no!'

'I'm sorry,' said the mayor, looking upon the captain with what appeared to be curiosity and pity.

'Do you have any pictures of the boy before today?' asked the captain.

After a moment a large oil portrait was carried forth, showing the son with a withered arm.

'My dear fellow!' The captain waved it away. 'Anybody can paint a picture. Paintings lie. I want a photograph of the boy.'

There was no photograph. Photography was not a known art in their society.

'Well,' sighed the captain, face twitching, 'let me talk to a few other citizens. We're getting nowhere.' He pointed at a woman. 'You.' She hesitated. 'Yes, you; come here,' ordered the captain. 'Tell me about this wonderful man you saw yesterday.'

The woman looked steadily at the captain. 'He walked among us and was very fine and good.'

'What colour were his eyes?'

'The colour of the sun, the colour of the sea, the colour of a flower, the colour of the mountains, the colour of the night.'

'That'll do.' The captain threw up his hands. 'See, Martin? Absolutely nothing. Some charlatan wanders through whispering sweet nothings in their ears and—'

'Please, stop it,' said Martin.

The captain stepped back. 'What?'

'You heard what I said,' said Martin. 'I like these people. I believe what they say. You're entitled to your opinion, but keep it to yourself, sir.'

'You can't talk to me this way,' shouted the captain.

'I've had enough of your high-handedness,' replied Martin. 'Leave these people alone. They've got something good and decent, and you come and foul up the nest and sneer at it. Well,

I've talked to them too. I've gone through the city and seen their faces, and they've got something you'll never have – a little simple faith, and they'll move mountains with it. You, you're boiled because someone stole your act, got here ahead and made you unimportant!'

'I'll give you five seconds to finish,' remarked the captain. 'I understand. You've been under a strain, Martin. Months of travelling in space, nostalgia, loneliness. And now, with this thing happening, I sympathize, Martin. I overlook your petty insubordination.'

'I don't overlook your petty tyranny,' replied Martin. 'I'm stepping out. I'm staying here.'

'You can't do that!'

'Can't I? Try and stop me. This is what I came looking for. I didn't know it, but this is it. This is for me. Take your filth somewhere else and foul up other nests with your doubt and your – scientific method!' He looked swiftly about. 'These people have had an experience, and you can't seem to get it through your head that it's really happened and we were lucky enough to almost arrive in time to be in on it.

'People on Earth have talked about this man for twenty centuries after he walked through the old world. We've all wanted to see him and hear him, and never had the chance. And now, today, we just missed seeing him by a few hours.'

Captain Hart looked at Martin's cheeks. 'You're crying like a baby. Stop it.'

'I don't care.'

'Well, I do. In front of these natives we're to keep up a front. You're overwrought. As I said, I forgive you.'

'I don't want your forgiveness.'

'You idiot. Can't you see this is one of Burton's tricks, to fool these people, to bilk them, to establish his oil and mineral concerns under a religious guise! You fool, Martin. You absolute fool! You should know Earthmen by now. They'll do anything – blaspheme, lie, cheat, steal, kill, to get their ends. Anything is fine if it works; the true pragmatist, that's Burton. You know him!'

The captain scoffed heavily. 'Come off it, Martin, admit it; this is the sort of scaly thing Burton might carry off, polish up these citizens and pluck them when they're ripe.'

'No,' said Martin, thinking of it.

The captain put his hand up. 'That's Burton. That's him. That's his dirt, that's his criminal way. I have to admire the old dragon. Flaming in here in a blaze and a halo and a soft word and a loving touch, with a medicated salve here and a healing ray there. That's Burton all right!'

'No.' Martin's voice was dazed. He covered his eyes. 'No, I won't believe it.'

'You don't want to believe.' Captain Hart kept at it. 'Admit it now. Admit it! It's just the thing Burton would do. Stop day-dreaming, Martin. Wake up! It's morning. This is a real world and we're real, dirty people – Burton the dirtiest of us all!'

Martin turned away.

'There, there, Martin,' said Hart, mechanically patting the man's back. 'I understand. Quite a shock for you. I know. A rotten shame, and all that. That Burton is a rascal. You go take it easy. Let me handle this.'

Martin walked off slowly toward the rocket.

Captain Hart watched him go. Then, taking a deep breath, he turned to the woman he had been questioning. 'Well. Tell me some more about this man. As you were saying, madam?'

Later the officers of the rocket ship ate supper on card tables outside. The captain correlated his data to a silent Martin who sat red-eyed and brooding over his meal.

'Interviewed three dozen people, all of them full of the same milk and hogwash,' said the captain. 'It's Burton's work all right, I'm positive. He'll be spilling back in here tomorrow or next week to consolidate his miracles and beat us out in our contracts. I think I'll stick on and spoil it for him.'

Martin glanced up sullenly. 'I'll kill him,' he said.

'No, now, Martin! There, there, boy.'

'I'll kill him – so help me, I will.'

'We'll put an anchor on his wagon. You have to admit he's clever. Unethical but clever.'

'He's dirty.'

'You must promise not to do anything violent.' Captain Hart checked his figures. 'According to this, there were thirty miracles of healing performed, a blind man restored to vision, a leper cured. Oh, Burton's efficient, give him that.'

A gong sounded. A moment later a man ran up. 'Captain, sir. A report! Burton's ship is coming down. Also the Ashley ship, sir!'

'See!' Captain Hart beat the table. 'Here come the jackals to the harvest! They can't wait to feed. Wait till I confront them. I'll make them cut me in on this feast – I will!'

Martin looked sick. He stared at the captain.

'Business, my dear boy, business,' said the captain.

Everybody looked up. Two rockets swung down out of the sky.

When the rockets landed they almost crashed.

'What's wrong with those fools?' cried the captain, jumping up. The men ran across the meadowlands to the steaming ships. The captain arrived. The airlock door popped open on Burton's ship.

A man fell out into their arms.

'What's wrong?' cried Captain Hart.

The man lay on the ground. They bent over him and he was burned, badly burned. His body was covered with wounds and scars and tissue that was inflamed and smoking. He looked up out of puffed eyes and his thick tongue moved in his split lips.

'What happened?' demanded the captain, kneeling down, shaking the man's arm.

'Sir, sir,' whispered the dying man. 'Forty-eight hours ago, back in Space Sector Seventy-nine DFS, off Planet One in this system, our ship, and Ashley's ship, ran into a cosmic storm, sir.' Liquid ran grey from the man's nostrils. Blood trickled from his mouth. 'Wiped out. All crew. Burton dead. Ashley died an hour ago. Only three survivors.'

'Listen to me!' shouted Hart, bending over the bleeding man. 'You didn't come to this planet before this very hour?'

Silence.

'Answer me!' cried Hart.

The dying man said, 'No. Storm. Burton dead two days ago. This first landing on any world in six months.'

'Are you sure?' shouted Hart, shaking violently, gripping the man in his hands. 'Are you sure?'

'Sure, sure,' mouthed the dying man.

'Burton died two days ago? You're positive?'

'Yes, yes,' whispered the man. His head fell forward. The man was dead.

The captain knelt beside the silent body. The captain's face twitched, the muscles jerking involuntarily. The other members of the crew stood behind him looking down. Martin waited. The captain asked to be helped to his feet, finally, and this was done. They stood looking at the city. 'That means—'

'That means?' said Martin.

'We're the only ones who've been here,' whispered Captain Hart. 'And that man—'

'What about that man, Captain?' asked Martin.

The captain's face twitched senselessly. He looked very old indeed, and grey. His eyes were glazed. He moved forward in the dry grass.

'Come along, Martin. Come along. Hold me up, for my sake, hold me. I'm afraid I'll fall. And hurry. We can't waste time—'

They moved, stumbling, toward the city, in the long dry grass, in the blowing wind.

Several hours later they were sitting in the mayor's auditorium. A thousand people had come and talked and gone. The captain had remained seated, his face haggard, listening, listening. There was so much light in the faces of those who came and testified and talked, he could not bear to see them. And all the while his hands travelled, on his knees, together; on his belt, jerking and quivering.

When it was over, Captain Hart turned to the mayor and with strange eyes said:

'But you must know where he went?'

'He didn't say where he was going,' replied the mayor.

'To one of the other nearby worlds?' demanded the captain.

'I don't know.'

'You must know.'

'Do you see him?' asked the mayor, indicating the crowd.

The captain looked. 'No.'

'Then he is probably gone,' said the mayor.

'Probably, probably!' cried the captain weakly. 'I've made a horrible mistake, and I want to see him now. Why, it just came to me, this is a most unusual thing in history. To be in on something like this. Why, the chances are one in billions we'd arrived at one certain planet among millions of planets the day after *he* came! You must know where he's gone!'

'Each finds him in his own way,' replied the mayor gently.

'You're hiding him.' The captain's face grew slowly ugly. Some of the old hardness returned in stages. He began to stand up.

'No,' said the mayor.

'You know where he is then?' The captain's fingers twitched at the leather holster on his right side.

'I couldn't tell you where he is, exactly,' said the mayor.

'I advise you to start talking,' and the captain took out a small steel gun.

'There's no way,' said the mayor, 'to tell you anything.'

'Liar!'

An expression of pity came into the mayor's face as he looked at Hart.

'You're very tired,' he said. 'You've travelled a long way and you belong to a tired people who've been without faith a long time, and you want to believe so much now that you're interfering with yourself. You'll only make it harder if you kill. You'll never find him that way.'

'Where'd he go? He told you; you know. Come on, tell me!' The captain waved the gun.

The mayor shook his head.

'Tell me! Tell me!'

The gun cracked once, twice. The mayor fell, his arm wounded.

Martin leaped forward. 'Captain!'

The gun flashed at Martin. 'Don't interfere.'

On the floor, holding his wounded arm, the mayor looked up.

'Put down your gun. You're hurting yourself. You've never believed, and now that you think you believe, you hurt people because of it.'

'I don't need you,' said Hart, standing over him. 'If I missed him by one day here, I'll go on to another world. And another and another. I'll miss him by half a day on the next planet, maybe, and a quarter of a day on the third planet, and two hours on the next, and an hour on the next, and half an hour on the next, and a minute on the next. But after that, one day I'll catch up with him! Do you hear that?' He was shouting now, leaning wearily over the man on the floor. He staggered with exhaustion. 'Come along, Martin.' He let the gun hang in his hand.

'No,' said Martin. 'I'm staying here.'

'You're a fool. Stay if you like. But I'm going on, with the others, as far as I can go.'

The mayor looked up at Martin. 'I'll be all right. Leave me. Others will tend my wounds.'

'I'll be back,' said Martin. 'I'll walk as far as the rocket.'

They walked with vicious speed through the city. One could see with what effort the captain struggled to show all the old iron, to keep himself going. When he reached the rocket he slapped the side of it with a trembling hand. He holstered his gun. He looked at Martin.

'Well, Martin?'

Martin looked at him. 'Well, Captain?'

The captain's eyes were on the sky. 'Sure you won't – come with – with me, eh?'

'No, sir.'

'It'll be a great adventure, by God. I know I'll find him.'

'You are set on it now, aren't you, sir?' asked Martin.

The captain's face quivered and his eyes closed. 'Yes.'

'There's one thing I'd like to know.'

'What?'

'Sir, when you find him – if you find him,' asked Martin, 'what will you ask of him?'

'Why—' The captain faltered, opening his eyes. His hands clenched and unclenched. He puzzled a moment and then broke into a strange smile. 'Why, I'll ask him for a little – peace and quiet.' He touched the rocket. 'It's been a long time, a long, long time since – since I relaxed.'

'Did you ever just try, Captain?'

'I don't understand,' said Hart.

'Never mind. So long, Captain.'

'Good-bye, Mr. Martin.'

The crew stood by the port. Out of their number only three were going on with Hart. Seven others were remaining behind, they said, with Martin.

Captain Hart surveyed them and uttered his verdict: 'Fools!'

He, last of all, climbed into the airlock, gave a brisk salute, laughed sharply. The door slammed.

The rocket lifted into the sky on a pillar of fire.

Martin watched it go far away and vanish.

At the meadow's edge the mayor, supported by several men, beckoned.

'He's gone,' said Martin, walking up.

'Yes, poor man, he's gone,' said the mayor. 'And he'll go on, planet after planet, seeking and seeking, and always and always he will be an hour late, or a half hour late, or ten minutes late, or a minute late. And finally he will miss out by only a few seconds. And when he has visited three hundred worlds and is seventy or eighty years old he will miss out by only a fraction of a second, and then a smaller fraction of a second. And he will go on and on, thinking to find that very thing which he left behind here, on this planet, in this city—'

Martin looked steadily at the mayor.

The mayor put out his hand. 'Was there ever any doubt of it?' He beckoned to the others and turned. 'Come along now. We mustn't keep him waiting.'

They walked into the city.

THE LONG RAIN

The rain continued. It was a hard rain, a perpetual rain, a sweating and steaming rain; it was a mizzle, a downpour, a fountain, a whipping at the eyes, an undertow at the ankles; it was a rain to drown all rains and the memory of rains. It came by the pound and the ton, it hacked at the jungle and cut the trees like scissors and shaved the grass and tunnelled the soil and moulted the bushes. It shrank men's hands into the hands of wrinkled apes; it rained a solid glassy rain, and it never stopped.

'How much farther, Lieutenant?'

'I don't know. A mile, ten miles, a thousand.'

'Aren't you sure?'

'How can I be sure?'

'I don't like this rain. If we only knew how far it is to the Sun Dome, I'd feel better.'

'Another hour or two from here.'

'You really think so, Lieutenant?'

'Of course.'

'Or are you lying to keep us happy?'

'I'm lying to keep you happy. Shut up!'

The two men sat together in the rain. Behind them sat two other men who were wet and tired and slumped like clay that was melting.

The lieutenant looked up. He had a face that once had been brown and now the rain had washed it pale, and the rain had washed the colour from his eyes and they were white, as were his teeth, and as was his hair. He was all white. Even his uniform was beginning to turn white, and perhaps a little green with fungus.

The lieutenant felt the rain on his cheeks. 'How many million years since the rain stopped raining here on Venus?'

'Don't be crazy,' said one of the two other men. 'It never

stops raining on Venus. It just goes on and on. I've lived here for ten years and I never saw a minute, or even a second, when it wasn't pouring.'

'It's like living under water,' said the the lieutenant, and rose up, shrugging his guns into place. 'Well, we'd better get going. We'll find that Sun Dome yet.'

'Or we won't find it,' said the cynic.

'It's an hour or so.'

'Now you're lying to me, Lieutenant.'

'No, now I'm lying to myself. This is one of those times when you've got to lie. I can't take much more of this.

They walked down the jungle trail, now and then looking at their compasses. There was no direction anywhere, only what the compass said. There was a grey sky and rain falling and jungle and a path, and, far back behind them somewhere, a rocket in which they had ridden and fallen. A rocket in which lay two of their friends, dead and dripping rain.

They walked in single file, not speaking. They came to a river which lay wide and flat and brown, flowing down to the great Single Sea. The surface of it was stippled in a billion places by the rain.

'All right, Simmons.'

The lieutenant nodded and Simmons took a small packet from his back which, with a pressure of hidden chemical, inflated into a large boat. The lieutenant directed the cutting of wood and the quick making of paddles and they set out into the river, paddling swiftly across the smooth surface in the rain.

The lieutenant felt the cold rain on his cheeks and on his neck and on his moving arms. The cold was beginning to seep into his lungs. He felt the rain on his ears, on his eyes, on his legs.

'I didn't sleep last night,' he said.

'Who could? Who has? When? How many nights *have* we slept? Thirty nights, thirty days! Who can sleep with rain slamming their head, banging away. . . . I'd give anything for a hat. Anything at all, just so it wouldn't hit my head any more. I get headaches. My head is sore; it hurts all the time.'

'I'm sorry I came to China,' said one of the others.

'First time I ever heard Venus called China.'

'Sure, China. Chinese water cure. Remember the old torture? Rope you against a wall. Drop one drop of water on your head every half-hour. You go crazy waiting for the next one. Well, that's Venus, but on a big scale. We're not made for water. You can't sleep, you can't breathe right, and you're crazy from just being soggy. If we'd been ready for a crash, we'd have brought waterproofed uniforms and hats. It's this beating rain on your head gets you, most of all. It's so heavy. It's like BB shot. I don't know how long I can take it.'

'Boy, me for the Sun Dome! The man who thought *them* up, thought of something.'

They crossed the river, and in crossing they thought of the Sun Dome, somewhere ahead of them, shining in the jungle rain. A yellow house, round and bright as the sun. A house fifteen feet high by one hundred feet in diameter, in which was warmth and quiet and hot food and freedom from rain. And in the centre of the Sun Dome, of course, was a sun. A small floating free globe of yellow fire, drifting in a space at the top of the building where you could look at it from where you sat, smoking or reading a book or drinking your hot chocolate crowned with marshmallow dollops. There it would be, the yellow sun, just the size of the Earth sun, and it was warm and continuous, and the rain world of Venus would be forgotten as long as they stayed in that house and idled their time.

The lieutenant turned and looked back at the three men using their oars and gritting their teeth. They were as white as mushroom, as white as he was. Venus bleached everything away in a few months. Even the jungle was an immense cartoon nightmare, for how could the jungle be green with no sun, with always rain falling and always dusk? The white, white jungle with the pale cheese-coloured leaves, and the earth carved of wet Camembert, and the tree boles like immense toadstools – Everything black and white. And how often could you see the soil itself? Wasn't it mostly a creek, a stream, a puddle, a pool, a lake, a river, and then, at last, the sea?

'Here we are!'

They leaped out on the farther shore, splashing and sending

up showers. The boat was deflated and stored in a cigarette packet. Then, standing on the rainy shore, they tried to light up a few smokes for themselves, and it was five minutes or so before, shuddering, they worked the inverted lighter and, cupping their hands, managed a few drags upon cigarettes that all too quickly were limp and beaten away from their lips by a sudden slap of rain.

They walked on.

'Wait just a moment,' said the lieutenant. 'I thought I saw something ahead.'

'The Sun Dome?'

'I'm not sure. The rain closed in again.'

Simmons began to run. 'The Sun Dome!'

'Come back, Simmons!'

'The Sun Dome!'

Simmons vanished in the rain. The others ran after him.

They found him in a little clearing, and they stopped and looked at him and what he had discovered.

The rocket ship.

It was lying where they had left it. Somehow they had circled back and were where they had started. In the ruin of the ship green fungus was growing up out of the mouths of the two dead men. As they watched, the fungus took flower, the petals broke away in the rain, and the fungus died.

'How did we do it?'

'An electrical storm must be nearby. Threw our compasses off. That explains it.'

'You're right.'

'What'll we do now?'

'Start out again.'

'Good lord, we're not any closer to anywhere!'

'Let's try to keep calm about it, Simmons.'

'Calm, calm! This rain's driving me wild!'

'We've enough food for another two days if we're careful.'

The rain danced on their skin, on their wet uniforms; the rain streamed from their noses and ears, from their fingers and knees. They looked like stone fountains frozen in the jungle, issuing forth water from every pore.

And, as they stood, from a distance they heard a roar.

And the monster came out of the rain.

The monster was supported upon a thousand electric blue legs. It walked swiftly and terribly. It struck down a leg with a driving blow. Everywhere a leg struck a tree fell and burned. Great whiffs of ozone filled the rainy air, and smoke blew away and was broken up by the rain. The monster was a half mile wide and a mile high and it felt the ground like a great blind thing. Sometimes, for a moment, it had no legs at all. And then, in an instant, a thousand whips would fall out of its belly, white-blue whips, to sting the jungle.

'There's the electrical storm,' said one of the men. 'There's the thing ruined our compasses. And it's coming this way.'

'Lie down, everyone,' said the lieutenant.

'Run!' cried Simmons.

'Don't be a fool. Lie down. It hits the highest points. We may get through unhurt. Lie down about fifty feet from the rocket. It may very well spend its force there and leave us be. Get down!'

The men flopped.

'Is it coming?' they asked each other, after a moment.

'Coming.'

'Is it nearer?'

'Two hundred yards off.'

'Nearer?'

'Here she is!'

The monster came and stood over them. It dropped down ten blue bolts of lightning which struck the rocket. The rocket flashed like a beaten gong and gave off a metal ringing. The monster let down fifteen more bolts which danced about in a ridiculous pantomime, feeling the jungle and the watery soil.

'No, no!' One of the men jumped up.

'Get down, you fool!' said the lieutenant.

'No!'

The lightning struck the rocket another dozen times. The lieutenant turned his head on his arm and saw the blue blazing flashes. He saw trees split and crumple into ruin. He saw the

monstrous dark cloud turn like a black disc overhead and hurl
down a hundred other poles of electricity.

The man who had leaped up was now running, like someone
in a great hall of pillars. He ran and dodged between the pillars
and then at last a dozen of the pillars slammed down and there
was the sound a fly makes when landing upon the grill wires of
an exterminator. The lieutenant remembered this from his
childhood on a farm. And there was a smell of a man burned to
a cinder.

The lieutenant lowered his head. 'Don't look up,' he told the
others. He was afraid that he too might run at any moment.

The storm above them flashed down another series of bolts
and then moved on away. Once again there was only the rain,
which rapidly cleared the air of the charred smell, and in a
moment the three remaining men were sitting and waiting for
the beat of their hearts to subside into quiet once more.

They walked over to the body, thinking that perhaps they
could still save the man's life. They couldn't believe that there
wasn't some way to help the man. It was the natural act of men
who have not accepted death until they have touched it and
turned it over and made plans to bury it or leave it there for
the jungle to bury in an hour of quick growth.

The body was twisted steel, wrapped in burned leather. It
looked like a wax dummy that had been thrown into an inciner-
tor and pulled out after the wax had sunk to the charcoal skeleton. Only the teeth were white, and they shone like a strange
white bracelet dropped half through a clenched black fist.

'He shouldn't have jumped up.' They said it almost at the
same time.

Even as they stood over the body it began to vanish, for
the vegetation was edging in upon it, little vines and ivy and
creepers, and even flowers for the dead.

At a distance the storm walked off on blue bolts of lightning
and was gone.

They crossed a river and a creek and a stream and a dozen
other rivers and creeks and streams. Before their eyes rivers

appeared, rushing, new rivers, while old rivers changed their courses – rivers the colour of mercury, rivers the colour of silver and milk.

They came to the sea.

The Single Sea. There was only one continent on Venus. This land was three thousand miles long by a thousand miles wide, and about this island was the Single Sea, which covered the entire raining planet. The Single Sea, which lay upon the pallid shore with little motion . . .

'This way.' The lieutenant nodded south. 'I'm sure there are two Sun Domes down that way.'

'While they were at it, why didn't they build a hundred more?'

'There're a hundred and twenty of them now, aren't there?'

'One hundred and twenty-six, as of last month. They tried to push a bill through Congress back on Earth a year ago to provide for a couple dozen more, but oh no, you know how *that* is. They'd rather a few men went crazy with the rain.'

They started south.

The lieutenent and Simmons and the third man, Pickard, walked in the rain, in the rain that fell heavily and lightly, heavily and lightly; in the rain that poured and hammered and did not stop falling upon the land and the sea and the walking people.

Simmons saw it first. 'There it is!'

'There's what?'

'The Sun Dome!'

The lieutenant blinked the water from his eyes and raised his hands to ward off the stinging blows of the rain.

At a distance there was a yellow glow on the edge of the jungle, by the sea. It was, indeed, the Sun Dome.

The men smiled at each other.'

'Looks like you were right, Lieutenant.'

'Luck.'

'Brother, that puts muscle in me, just seeing it. Come on! Last one there's a son-of-a-bitch!' Simmons began to trot. The others automatically fell in with this, gasping, tired, but keeping pace.

'A big pot of coffee for me,' panted Simmons, smiling. 'And a pan of cinnamon buns, by God! And just lie there and let the old sun hit you. The guy that invented the Sun Domes, he should have got a medal!'

They ran faster. The yellow glow grew brighter.

'Guess a lot of men went crazy before they figured out the cure. Think it'd be obvious! Right off.' Simmons panted the words in cadence to his running. 'Rain, rain! Years ago. Found a friend. Of mine. Out in the jungle. Wandering around. In the rain. Saying over and over, "Don't know enough, to come in, outta the rain. Don't know enough, to come in, outta the rain. Don't know enough—" On and on. Like that. Poor crazy bastard.'

'Save your breath!'

They ran.

They all laughed. They reached the door of the Sun Dome, laughing.

Simmons yanked the door wide. 'Hey!' he yelled. 'Bring on the coffee and buns!'

There was no reply.

They stepped through the door.

The Sun Dome was empty and dark. There was no synthetic yellow sun floating in a high gaseous whisper at the centre of the blue ceiling. There was no food waiting. It was cold as a vault. And through a thousand holes which had been newly punctured in the ceiling water streamed, the rain fell down, soaking into the thick rugs and the heavy modern furniture and splashing on the glass tables. The jungle was growing up like a moss in the room, on top of the book cases and the divans. The rain slashed through the holes and fell upon the three men's faces.

Pickard began to laugh quietly.

'Shut up, Pickard!'

'Ye gods, look what's here for us – no food, no sun, nothing. The Venusians – they did it! Of course!'

Simmons nodded, with the rain funnelling down on his face. The water ran in his silvered hair and on his white eyebrows. 'Every once in a while the Venusians come up out of the sea and attack a Sun Dome. They know if they ruin the Sun Domes they can ruin us.'

'But aren't the Sun Domes protected with guns?'

'Sure.' Simmons stepped aside to a place that was relatively dry. 'But it's been five years since the Venusians tried anything. Defence relaxes. They caught this Dome unaware.'

'Where are the bodies?'

'The Venusians took them all down into the sea. I hear they have a delightful way of drowning you. It takes about eight hours to drown the way they work it. Really delightful.'

'I bet there isn't any food here at all.' Pickard laughed.

The lieutenant frowned at him, nodded at him so Simmons could see. Simmons shook his head and went back to a room at one side of the oval chamber. The kitchen was strewn with soggy loaves of bread, and meat that had grown a faint green fur. Rain came through a hundred holes in the kitchen roof.

'Brilliant.' The lieutenant glanced up at the holes. 'I don't suppose we can plug up all those holes and get snug here.'

'Without food, sir?' Simmons snorted. 'I notice the sun machine's torn apart. Our best bet is to make our way to the next Sun Dome. How far is that from here?'

'Not far. As I recall, they built two rather close together here. Perhaps if we waited here, a rescue mission from the other might—'

'It's probably been here and gone already, some days ago. They'll send a crew to repair this place in about six months, when they get the money from Congress. I don't think we'd better wait.'

'All right then, we'll eat what's left of our rations and get on to the next Dome.'

Pickard said, 'If only the rain wouldn't hit my head, just for a few minutes. If I could only remember what it's like not to be bothered.' He put his hands on his skull and held it tight. 'I remember when I was in school a bully used to sit in back of me and pinch me and pinch me and pinch me every five minutes, all day long. He did that for weeks and months. My arms were sore and black and blue all the time. And I thought I'd go crazy from being pinched. One day I must have gone a little mad from being hurt and hurt, and I turned around and took a metal tri-square I used in mechanical drawing and I almost killed that bastard. I almost cut his lousy head off. I almost took his eye out before they dragged me out of the room, and I kept yelling, "Why don't he leave me alone? Why don't he leave me alone?" Brother!' His hands clenched the bone of his head, shaking, tightening, his eyes shut. 'But what do I do *now*? Who do I hit, who do I tell to lay off, stop bothering me, this damn rain, like the pinching, always *on* you, that's all you hear, that's all you feel!'

'We'll be at the other Sun Dome by four this afternoon.'

'Sun Dome? Look at this one! What if all the Sun Domes on Venus are gone? What then? What if there are holes in all the ceilings, and the rain coming in!'

'We'll have to chance it.'

'I'm tired of chancing it. All I want is a roof and some quiet. I want to be alone.'

'That's only eight hours off, if you hold on.'

'Don't worry, I'll hold on all right.' And Pickard laughed, not looking at them.

'Let's eat,' said Simmons, watching him.

They set off down the coast, southward again. After four hours they had to cut inland to go around a river that was a mile wide and so swift it was not navigable by boat. They had to walk inland six miles to a place where the river boiled out of the earth, suddenly, like a mortal wound. In the rain, they walked on solid ground and returned to the sea.

'I've got to sleep,' said Pickard at last. He slumped. 'Haven't slept in four weeks. Tried, but couldn't. Sleep here.'

The sky was getting darker. The night of Venus was setting in and it was so completely black that it was dangerous to move. Simmons and the lieutenant fell to their knees also, and the lieutenant said, 'All right, we'll see what we can do. We've tried it before, but I don't know. Sleep doesn't seem one of the things you can get in this weather.'

They lay out full, propping their heads up so the water wouldn't come to their mouths, and they closed their eyes.

The lieutenant twitched.

He did not sleep.

There were things that crawled on his skin. Things grew upon him in layers. Drops fell and touched other drops and they became streams that trickled over his body, and while these moved down his flesh, the small growths of the forest took root in his clothing. He felt the ivy cling and make a second garment over him; he felt the small flowers bud and open and petal away, and still the rain pattered on his body and on his head. In the luminous night – for the vegetation glowed in the darkness – he could see the other two men outlined, like logs that had fallen and taken upon themselves velvet coverings of grass and flowers. The rain hit his face. He covered his face with his hands. The rain hit his neck. He turned over on his stomach in the mud, on the rubbery plants, and the rain hit his back and hit his legs.

Suddenly he leaped up and began to brush the water from himself. A thousand hands were touching him and he no longer wanted to be touched. He no longer could stand being touched. He floundered and struck something else and knew that it was Simmons, standing up in the rain, sneezing moisture, coughing and choking. And then Pickard was up, shouting, running about.

'Wait a minute, Pickard!'

'Stop it, stop it!' Pickard screamed. He fired off his gun six times at the night sky. In the flashes of powdery illumination they could see armies of raindrops, suspended as in a vast motionless amber, for an instant, hesitating as if shocked by the explosion, fifteen billion droplets, fifteen billion tears, fifteen billion ornaments, jewels standing out against a white velvet viewing board. And then, with the light gone, the drops which had waited to have their pictures taken, which had suspended their downward rush, fell upon them, stinging, in an insect cloud of coldness and pain.

'Stop it! Stop it!'

'Pickard!'

But Pickard was only standing now, alone. When the lieutenant switched on a small hand lamp and played it over Pickard's wet face, the eyes of the man were dilated, and his mouth was open, his face turned up, so the water hit and splashed on his tongue, and hit and drowned the wide eyes, and bubbled in a whispering froth on the nostrils.

'Pickard!'

The man would not reply. He simply stood there for a long while with the bubbles of rain breaking out in his whitened hair and manacles of rain jewels dripping from his wrists and his neck.

'Pickard! We're leaving. We're going on. Follow us.'

The rain dripped from Pickard's ears.

'Do you hear me, Pickard!'

It was like shouting down a well.

'Pickard!'

'Leave him alone,' said Simmons.

'We can't go on without him.'

'What'll we do, carry him?' Simmons spat. 'He's no good to us or himself. You know what he'll do? He'll just stand here and drown.'

'What?'

'You ought to know that by now. Don't you know the story? He'll just stand here with his head up and let the rain come in his nostrils and his mouth. He'll breathe the water.'

'No.'

'That's how they found General Mendt that time. Sitting on a rock with his head back, breathing the rain. His lungs were full of water.'

The lieutenant turned the light back to the unblinking face. Pickard's nostrils gave off a tiny whispering wet sound.

'Pickard!' The lieutenant slapped the face.

'He can't even feel you,' said Simmons. 'A few days in this rain and you don't have any face or any legs or hands.'

The lieutenant looked at his own hand in horror. He could no longer feel it.

'But we can't leave Pickard here.'

'I'll show you what we can do.' Simmons fired his gun.

Pickard fell into the raining earth.

Simmons said, 'Don't move, Lieutenant. I've got my gun ready for you too. Think it over; he would only have stood or sat there and drowned. It's quicker this way.'

The lieutenant blinked at the body. 'But you killed him.'

'Yes, because he'd have killed us by being a burden. You saw his face. Insane.'

After a moment the lieutenant nodded. 'All right.'

They walked off into the rain.

It was dark and their hand lamps threw a beam that pierced the rain for only a few feet. After a half hour they had to stop and sit through the rest of the night, aching with hunger, waiting for the dawn to come; when it did come it was grey and continually raining as before, and they began to walk again.

'We've miscalculated,' said Simmons.

'No. Another hour.'

'Speak louder. I can't hear you.' Simmons stopped and smiled. 'By Christ,' he said, and touched his ears. 'My ears. They've gone out on me. All the rain pouring finally numbed me right down to the bone.'

'Can't you hear anything?' said the lieutenant.

'What?' Simmons's eyes were puzzled.

'Nothing. Come on.'

'I think I'll wait here. You go on ahead.'

'You can't do that.'

'I can't hear you. You go on. I'm tired. I don't think the Sun Dome is down this way. And, if it is, it's probably got holes in the roof, like the last one. I think I'll just sit here.'

'Get up from there!'

'So long, Lieutenant.'

'You can't give up now.'

'I've got a gun here that says I'm staying. I just don't give a damn any more. I'm not crazy yet, but I'm the next thing to it. I don't want to go out that way. As soon as you get out of sight I'm going to use this gun on myself.'

'Simmons!'

'You said my name. I can read that much off your lips.'

'Simmons.'

'Look, it's a matter of time. Either I die now or in a few

hours. Wait'll you get to that next Dome, if you ever get there, and find rain coming in through the roof. Won't that be nice?

The lieutenant waited and then splashed off in the rain. He turned and called back once, but Simmons was only sitting there with the gun in his hands, waiting for him to get out of sight. He shook his head and waved the lieutenant on.

The lieutenant didn't even hear the sound of the gun.

He began to eat the flowers as he walked. They stayed down for a time, and weren't poisonous; neither were they particularly sustaining, and he vomited them up, sickly, a minute or so later.

Once he took some leaves and tried to make himself a hat, but he had tried that before, the rain melted the leaves from his head. Once picked, the vegetation rotted quickly and fell away into grey masses in his fingers.

'Another five minutes,' he told himself. 'Another five minutes and then I'll walk into the sea and keep walking. We weren't made for this; no Earthman was or ever will be able to take it. Your nerves, your nerves.'

He floundered his way through a sea of slush and foliage and came to a small hill.

At a distance there was a faint yellow smudge in the cold veils of water.

The next Sun Dome.

Through the trees, a long round yellow building, far away. For a moment he only stood, swaying, looking at it.

He began to run and then he slowed down, for he was afraid. He didn't call out. What if it's the same one? What if it's the dead Sun Dome, with no sun in it? he thought.

He slipped and fell. Lie here, he thought, it's the wrong one. Lie here. It's no use. Drink all you want.

But he managed to climb to his feet again and crossed several creeks, and the yellow light grew very bright, and he began to run again, his feet crashing into mirrors and glass, his arms flailing at diamonds and precious stones.

He stood before the yellow door. The printed letters over it said THE SUN DOME. He put his numb hand up to feel it. Then he twisted the doorknob and stumbled in.

He stood for a moment looking about. Behind him the rain whirled at the door. Ahead of him, upon a low table, stood a silver pot of hot chocolate, steaming, and a cup, full, with a marshmallow in it. And beside that, on another tray, stood thick sandwiches of rich chicken meat and fresh-cut tomatoes and green onions. And on a rod just before his eyes was a great thick green Turkish towel, and a bin, in which to throw wet clothes, and, to his right, a small cubicle in which heat rays might dry you instantly. And upon a chair, a fresh change of uniform, waiting for anyone – himself, or any lost one – to make use of it. And farther over, coffee in steaming copper urns, and a phonograph from which music was playing quietly, and books bound in red and brown leather. And near the books a cot, a soft deep cot upon which one might lie, exposed and bare, to drink in the rays of the one great bright thing which dominated the long room.

He put his hands to his eyes. He saw other men moving toward him, but said nothing to them. He waited, and opened his eyes, and looked. The water from his uniform pooled at his feet, and he felt it drying from his hair and his face and his chest and his arms and his legs.

He was looking at the sun.

It hung in the centre of the room, large and yellow and warm. It made not a sound, and there was no sound in the room. The door was shut and the rain only a memory to his tingling body. The sun hung high in the blue sky of the room, warm, hot, yellow, and very fine.

He walked forward, tearing off his clothes as he went.

USHER II

' "During the whole of a dull, dark, and soundless day in the autumn of the year, when the clouds hung oppressively low in the heavens, I had been passing alone, on horseback, through a singularly dreary tract of country, and at length found myself, as the shades of evening drew on, within view of the melancholy House of Usher. . . ." '

Mr. William Stendahl paused in his quotation. There, upon a low black hill, stood the House, its cornerstone bearing the inscription 2005 A.D.

Mr. Bigelow, the architect, said, 'It's completed. Here's the key, Mr. Stendahl.'

The two men stood together silently in the quiet autumn afternoon. Blueprints rustled on the raven grass at their feet.

'The House of Usher,' said Mr. Stendahl with pleasure. 'Planned, built, bought, paid for. Wouldn't Mr. Poe be *delighted*!'

Mr. Bigelow squinted. 'Is it everything you wanted, sir?'

'Yes!'

'Is the colour right? Is it *desolate* and *terrible*?'

'Very desolate, very terrible!'

'The walls are — *bleak*?'

'Amazingly so!'

'The tarn, is it "black and lurid" enough?'

'Most incredibly black and lurid.'

'And the sedge — we've dyed it, you know — is it the proper grey and ebon?'

'Hideous!'

Mr. Bigelow consulted his architectural plans. From these he quoted in part: 'Does the whole structure cause an "iciness, a sickening of the heart, a dreariness of thought"? The House, the lake, the land, Mr. Stendahl?'

'Mr. Bigelow, it's worth every penny! My God, it's beautiful!'

'Thank you. I had to work in total ignorance. Thank the Lord you had your own private rockets or we'd never have been allowed to bring most of the equipment through. You notice, it's always twilight here, this land, always October, barren, sterile, dead. It took a bit of doing. We killed everything. Ten thousand tons of DDT. Not a snake, frog, or Martian fly left! Twilight always, Mr. Stendahl; I'm proud of that. There are machines, hidden, which blot out the sun. It's always properly "dreary".'

Stendahl drank it in, the dreariness, the oppression, the foetid vapours, the whole 'atmosphere', so delicately contrived and fitted. And that House! That crumbling horror, that evil lake, the fungi, the extensive decay! Plastic or otherwise, who could guess?

He looked at the autumn sky. Somewhere above, beyond, far off, was the sun. Somewhere it was the month of April on the planet Mars, a yellow month with a blue sky. Somewhere above, the rockets burned down to civilize a beautifully dead planet. The sound of their screaming passage was muffled by this dim, sound-proofed world, this ancient autumn world.

'Now that my job's done,' said Mr. Bigelow uneasily, 'I feel free to ask what you're going to do with all this.'

'With Usher? Haven't you guessed?'

'No.'

'Does the name Usher mean nothing to you?'

'Nothing.'

'Well, what about *this* name: Edgar Allan Poe?'

Mr. Bigelow shook his head.

'Of course.' Stendahl snorted delicately, a combination of dismay and contempt. 'How could I expect you to know blessed Mr. Poe? He died a long while ago, before Lincoln. All of his books were burned in the Great Fire. That's thirty years ago – 1975.'

'Ah,' said Mr. Bigelow wisely. 'One of *those*!'

'Yes, one of those, Bigelow. He and Lovecraft and Hawthorne and Ambrose Bierce and all the tales of terror and fan-

tasy and horror and, for that matter, tales of the future, were
burned. Heartlessly. They passed a law. Oh, it started very
small. In 1959 and '60 it was a grain of sand. They began by
controlling books of cartoons and then detective books and, of
course, films, one way or another, one group or another, politi-
cal bias, religious prejudice, union pressures; there was always
a minority afraid of something, and a great majority afraid of
the dark, afraid of the future, afraid of the past, afraid of the
present, afraid of themselves and shadows of themselves.'

'I see.'

'Afraid of the word "politics" (which eventually became a
synonym for Communism among the more reactionary ele-
ments, so I hear, and it was worth your life to use the word!),
and with a screw tightened here, a bolt fastened there, a push, a
pull, a yank, art and literature were soon like a great twine of
taffy strung about, being twisted in braids and tied in knots and
thrown in all directions, until there was no more resiliency and
no more savour to it. Then the film cameras chopped short and
the theatres turned dark, and the printing presses trickled down
from a great Niagara of reading matter to a mere innocuous
dripping of "pure" material. Oh, the word "escape" was rad-
ical, too, I tell you!'

'Was it?'

'It was! Every man, they said, must face reality. Must face
the Here and Now! Everything that was *not so* must go. All the
beautiful literary lies and flights of fancy must be shot in mid-
air! So they lined them up against a library wall one Sunday
morning thirty years ago, in 1975; they lined them up, St.
Nicholas and the Headless Horseman and Snow White and
Rumpelstiltskin and Mother Goose – oh, what a wailing! – and
shot them down, and burned the paper castles and the fairy
frogs and old kings and the people who lived happily ever
after (for of course it was a fact that *nobody* lived happily ever
after), and Once Upon A Time became No More! And they
spread the ashes of the Phantom Rickshaw with the rubble of
the Land of Oz; they filleted the bones of Glinda the Good and
Ozma and shattered Polychrome in a spectroscope and served
Jack Pumpkinhead with meringue at the Biologists' Ball! The

Beanstalk died in a bramble of red tape! Sleeping Beauty awoke at the kiss of a scientist and expired at the fatal puncture of his syringe. And they made Alice drink something from a bottle which reduced her to a size where she could no longer cry "Curiouser and curiouser", and they gave the Looking Glass one hammer blow to smash it and every Red King and Oyster away!'

He clenched his fists. Lord, how immediate it was! His face was red and he was gasping for breath.

As for Mr. Bigelow, he was astounded at this long explosion. He blinked and at last said, 'Sorry. Don't know what you're talking about. Just names to me. From what I hear, the Burning was a good thing.'

'Get out!' screamed Stendahl. 'You've done your job, now let me alone, you idiot!'

Mr. Bigelow summoned his carpenters and went away.

Mr. Stendahl stood alone before his House.

'Listen here,' he said to the unseen rockets. 'I came to Mars to get away from you Clean-Minded people, but you're flocking in thicker every day, like flies to offal. So I'm going to show you. I'm going to teach you a fine lesson for what you did to Mr. Poe on Earth. As of this day, beware. The House of Usher is open for business!'

He pushed a fist at the sky.

The rocket landed. A man stepped out jauntily. He glanced at the House, and his grey eyes were displeased and vexed. He strode across the moat to confront the small man there.

'Your name Stendahl?'

'Yes.'

'I'm Garrett, Investigator of Moral Climates.'

'So you finally got to Mars, you Moral Climate people? I wondered when you'd appear.'

'We arrived last week. We'll soon have things as neat and tidy as Earth.' The man waved an identification card irritably toward the House. 'Suppose you tell me about that place, Stendahl?'

'It's a haunted castle, if you like.'

'I don't like, Stendahl, I *don't* like. The sound of that word "haunted".'

'Simple enough. In this year of our Lord 2005 I have built a mechanical sanctuary. In it copper bats fly on electronic beams, brass rats scuttle in plastic cells, robot skeletons dance; robot vampires, harlequins, wolves, and white phantoms, compounded of chemical and ingenuity, live here.'

'That's what I was afraid of,' said Garrett, smiling quietly. 'I'm afraid we're going to have to tear your place down.'

'I knew you'd come out as soon as you discovered what went on.'

'I'd have come sooner, but we at Moral Climates wanted to be sure of your intentions before we moved in. We can have the Dismantlers and Burning Crew here by supper. By midnight your place will be razed to the cellar. Mr. Stendahl, I consider you somewhat of a fool, sir. Spending hard-earned money on a folly. Why, it must have cost you three million dollars—'

'Four million! But, Mr. Garrett, I inherited twenty-five million when very young. I can afford to throw it about. Seems a dreadful shame, though, to have the House finished only an hour and have you race out with your Dismantlers. Couldn't you possibly let me play with my Toy for just, well, twenty-four hours?'

'You know the law. Strict to the letter. No books, no houses, nothing to be produced which in any way suggests ghosts, vampires, fairies, or any creature of the imagination.'

'You'll be burning Babbits next!'

'You've caused us a lot of trouble, Mr. Stendahl. It's in the record. Twenty years ago. On Earth. You and your library.'

'Yes, me and my library. And a few others like me. Oh, Poe's been forgotten for many years now, and Oz and the other creatures. But I had my little cache. We had our libraries, a few private citizens, until you sent your men around with torches and incinerators and tore my fifty thousand books up and burned them. Just as you put a stake through the heart of Halloween and told your film producers that if they made anything at all they would have to make and remake Ernest Hemingway. My God, how many times have I seen *For Whom the Bell Tolls* done! Thirty different versions. All realistic. Oh, realism! Oh, here, oh, now, oh hell!'

'It doesn't pay to be bitter!'

'Mr. Garrett, you must turn in a full report, mustn't you?'

'Yes.'

'Then, for curiosity's sake, you'd better come in and look around. It'll take only a minute.'

'All right. Lead the way. And no tricks. I've a gun with me.'

The door to the House of Usher creaked wide. A moist wind issued forth. There was an immense sighing and moaning, like a subterranean bellows breathing in the lost catacombs.

A rat pranced across the floor stones. Garrett, crying out, gave it a kick. It fell over, the rat did, and from its nylon fur streamed an incredible horde of metal fleas.

'Amazing!' Garrett bent to see.

An old witch sat in a niche, quivering her wax hands over some orange-and-blue tarot cards. She jerked her head and hissed through her toothless mouth at Garrett, tapping her greasy cards.

'Death!' she cried.

'Now *that's* the sort of thing I mean,' said Garrett. 'Deplorable!'

'I'll let you burn her personally.'

'Will you, really?' Garrett was pleased. Then he frowned. 'I must say you're taking this all so well.'

'It was enough just to be able to create this place. To be able to say I did it. To say I nurtured a medieval atmosphere in a modern, incredulous world.'

'I've a somewhat reluctant admiration for your genius myself, sir.' Garrett watched a mist drift by, whispering and whispering, shaped like a beautiful and nebulous woman. Down a moist corridor a machine whirled. Like the stuff from a cotton-candy centrifuge, mists sprang up and floated, murmuring, in the silent hall.

An ape appeared out of nowhere.

'Hold on!' cried Garrett.

'Don't be afraid.' Stendahl tapped the animal's black chest.

'A robot. Copper skeleton and all, like the witch. See?' He stroked the fur, and under it metal tubing came to light.

'Yes.' Garrett put out a timid hand to pet the thing. 'But why, Mr. Stendahl why all *this*? What obsessed you?'

'Bureaucracy, Mr. Garrett. But I haven't time to explain. The government will discover soon enough.' He nodded to the ape. 'All right. *Now*.'

The ape killed Mr. Garrett.

'Are we almost ready, Pikes?'

Pikes looked up from the table. 'Yes, sir.'

'You've done a splendid job.'

'Well, I'm paid for it, Mr. Stendahl,' said Pikes softly as he lifted the plastic eyelid of the robot and inserted the glass eye-ball to fasten the rubberoid muscles neatly. 'There.'

'The spitting image of Mr. Garrett.'

'What do we do with him, sir?' Pikes nodded at the slab where the real Mr. Garret lay dead.

'Better burn him, Pikes. We wouldn't want two Mr. Gar-retts, would we?'

Pikes wheeled Mr. Garrett to the brick incinerator. 'Goodbye.' He pushed Mr. Garrett in and slammed the door.

Stendahl confronted the robot Garrett. 'You have your orders, Garrett?'

'Yes, sir.' The robot sat up. 'I'm to return to Moral Climates. I'll file a complementary report. Delay action for at least forty-eight hours. Say I'm investigating more fully.'

'Right, Garrett. Good-bye.'

The robot hurried out to Garrett's rocket, got in, and flew away.

Stendahl turned. 'Now, Pikes, we send the remainder of the invitations for tonight. I think we'll have a jolly time, don't you?'

'Considering we waited twenty years, quite jolly!'

They winked at each other.

Seven o'clock. Stendahl studied his watch. Almost time. He

twirled the sherry glass in his hand. He sat quietly. Above him,
among the oaken beams, the bats, their delicate copper bodies
hidden under rubber flesh, blinked at him and shrieked. He
raised his glass to them. 'To our success.' Then he leaned back,
closed his eyes, and considered the entire affair. How he would
savour this in his old age. This paying back of the antiseptic
government for its literary terrors and conflagrations. Oh, how
the anger and hatred had grown in him through the years. Oh,
how the plan had taken a slow shape in his numbed mind, until
that day three years ago when he had met Pikes.

Ah yes, Pikes. Pikes with the bitterness in him as deep as a
black, charred well of green acid. Who was Pikes? Only the
greatest of them all! Pikes, the man of ten thousand faces, a
fury, a smoke, a blue fog, a white rain, a bat, a gargoyle, a
monster, that was Pikes! Better than Lon Chaney, the father?
Stendahl ruminated. Night after night he had watched Chaney
in the old, old films. Yes, better than Chaney. Better than that
other ancient mummer? What was his name? Karloff? Far
better! Lugosi? The comparison was odious! No, there was
only one Pikes, and he was a man stripped of his fantasies now,
no place on Earth to go, no one to show off to. Forbidden even
to perform for himself before a mirror!

Poor impossible, defeated Pikes! How must it have felt,
Pikes, the night they seized your films, like entrails yanked
from the camera, out of your guts, clutching them in rolls and
wads to stuff them up a stove to burn away! Did it feel as bad
as having some fifty thousand books annihilated with no re-
compense? Yes. Yes. Stendahl felt his hands grow cold with the
senseless anger. So what more natural than they would one day
talk over endless coffee-pots into innumerable midnights, and
out of all the talk and the bitter brewings would come – the
House of Usher.

A great church bell rang. The guests were arriving.

Smiling, he went to greet them.

Full grown without memory, the robots waited. In green
silks the colour of forest pools, in silks the colour of frog and

fern, they waited. In yellow hair the colour of the sun and sand, the robots waited. Oiled, with the tube bones cut from bronze and sunk in gelatin, the robots lay. In coffins for the not dead and not alive, in planked boxes, the metronomes waited to be set in motion. There was a smell of lubrication and lathed brass. There was a silence of the tomb yard. Sexed but sexless, the robots. Named but unnamed, and borrowing from humans everything but humanity, the robots stared at the nailed lids of their labelled F.O.B. boxes, in a death that was not even a death, for there had never been a life. And now there was a vast screaming of yanked nails. Now there was a lifting of lids. Now there were shadows on the boxes and the pressure of a hand squirting oil from a can. Now one clock was set in motion, a faint ticking. Now another and another, until this was an immense clock shop, purring. The marble eyes rolled wide their rubber lids. The nostrils winked. The robots, clothed in hair of ape and white of rabbit, arose: Tweedledum following Tweedledee, Mock-Turtle, Dormouse, drowned bodies from the sea compounded of salt and whiteweed, swaying; hanging blue-throated men with turned-up clam-flesh eyes, and creatures of ice and burning tinsel, loam-dwarfs and pepper-elves, Tik-Tok, Ruggedo, St. Nicholas with a self-made snow-flurry blowing on before him, Bluebeard with whiskers like acetylene flame, and sulphur clouds from which green fire snouts protruded, and, in scaly and gigantic serpentine, a dragon with a furnace in its belly reeled out the door with a scream, a tick, a bellow, a silence, a rush, a wind. Ten thousand lids fell back. The clock shop moved out into Usher. The night was enchanted.

A warm breeze came over the land. The guest rockets, burning the sky and turning the weather from autumn to spring, arrived.

The men stepped out in evening clothes and the women stepped out after them, their hair coiffed up in elaborate detail.

'So *that's* Usher!'

'But where's the door?'

At this moment Stendahl appeared. The women laughed and chattered. Mr. Stendah raised a hand to quiet them. Turning, he looked up to a high castle window and called:

'Rapunzel, Rapunzel, let down your hair.'

And from above, a beautiful maiden leaned out upon the night wind and let down her golden hair. And the hair twined and blew and became a ladder upon which the guests might ascend, laughing, into the House.

What eminent sociologists! What clever psychologists! What tremendously important politicians, bacteriologists, and neurologists! There they stood, within the dank walls.

'Welcome, all of you!'

Mr. Tyron, Mr. Owen, Mr. Dunne, Mr. Lang, Mr. Steffens, Mr. Fletcher, and a double-dozen more.

'Come in, come in!'

Miss Gibbs, Miss Pope, Miss Churchill, Miss Blunt, Miss Drummond, and a score of other women, glittering.

Eminent, eminent people, one and all, members of the Society for the Prevention of Fantasy, advocators of the banishment of Halloween and Guy Fawkes, killers of bats, burners of books, bearers of torches; good clean citizens, every one, who had waited until the rough men had come up and buried the Martians and cleansed the cities and built the towns and repaired the highways and made everything safe. And then, with everything well on its way to Safety, the Spoil-Funs, the people with mercurochrome for blood and iodine-coloured eyes, came now to set up their Moral Climates and dole out goodness to everyone. And they were his friends! Yes, carefully, carefully, he had met and befriended each of them on Earth in the last year!

'Welcome to the vasty halls of Death!' he cried.

'Hello, Stendahl, what *is* all this?'

'You'll see. Everyone off with their clothes. You'll find booths to one side there. Change into costumes you find there. Men on this side, women on that.'

The people stood uneasily about.

'I don't know if we should stay,' said Miss Pope. 'I don't like the looks of this. It verges on – blasphemy.'

'Nonsense, a *costume* ball.'

'Seems quite illegal.' Mr. Steffens sniffed about.

'Come off it.' Stendahl laughed. 'Enjoy yourselves. Tomorrow it'll be a ruin. Get in the booths!'

The House blazed with life and colour; harlequins rang by with belled caps and white mice danced miniature quadrilles to the music of dwarfs who tickled tiny fiddles with tiny bows, and flags rippled from scorched beams while bats flew in clouds about gargoyle mouths which spouted down wine, cool, wild, and foaming. A creek wandered through the seven rooms of the masked ball. Guests sipped and found it to be sherry. Guests poured from the booths, transformed from one age into another, their faces covered with dominoes, the very act of putting on a mask revoking all their licences to pick a quarrel with fantasy and horror. The women swept about in red gowns, laughing. The men danced them attendance. And on the walls were shadows with no people to throw them, and here or there were mirrors in which no image showed. 'All of us vampires!' laughed Mr. Fletcher. 'Dead!'

There were seven rooms, each a different colour, one blue, one purple, one green, one orange, another white, the sixth violet, and the seventh shrouded in black velvet. And in the black room was an ebony clock which struck the hour loud. And through these rooms the guests ran, drunk at last, among the robot fantasies, amid the Dormice and Mad Hatters, the Trolls and Giants, the Black Cats and White Queens, and under their dancing feet the floor gave off the massive pumping beat of a hidden and tell-tale heart.

'Mr. Stendahl!'

A whisper.

'Mr. Stendahl!'

A monster with the face of Death stood at his elbow. It was Pikes. 'I must see you alone.'

'What is it?'

'Here.' Pikes held out a skeleton hand. In it were a few half-melted, charred wheels, nuts, cogs, bolts.

Stendahl looked at them for a long moment. Then he drew Pikes into a corridor. 'Garrett?' he whispered.

Pikes nodded. 'He sent a robot in his place. Cleaning out the incinerator a moment ago, I found these.'

They both stared at the fateful cogs for a time.

'This means the police will be here any minute,' said Pikes. 'Our plan will be ruined.'

'I don't know.' Stendahl glanced in at the whirling yellow and blue and orange people. The music swept through the misting halls. 'I should have guessed Garrett wouldn't be fool enough to come in person. But wait!'

'What's the matter?'

'Nothing. There's nothing the matter. Garrett sent a robot to us. Well, we sent one back. Unless he checks closely, he won't notice the switch.'

'Of course!'

'Next time he'll come *himself*. Now that he thinks it's safe. Why, he might be at the door any minute, in *person*! More wine, Pikes!'

The great bell rang.

'There he is now, I'll bet you. Go let Mr. Garrett in.'

Rapunzel let down her golden hair.

'Mr. Stendahl?'

'Mr. Garrett. The *real* Mr. Garrett?'

'The same.' Garrett eyed the dank walls and the whirling people. 'I thought I'd better come see for myself. You can't depend on robots. Other people's robots, especially. I also took the precaution of summoning the Dismantlers. They'll be here in one hour to knock the props out from under this horrible place.'

Stendahl bowed. 'Thanks for telling me.' He waved his hand. 'In the meantime, you might as well enjoy this. A little wine?'

'No, thank you. What's going on? How low can a man sink?'

'See for yourself, Mr. Garrett.'

'Murder,' said Garrett.

'Murder most foul,' said Stendahl.

A woman screamed. Miss Pope ran up, her face the colour of cheese. 'The most horrid thing just happened! I saw Miss Blunt strangled by an ape and stuffed up a chimney!'

They looked and saw the long yellow hair trailing down from the flue. Garrett cried out.

'Horrid!' sobbed Miss Pope, and then ceased crying. She blinked and turned. 'Miss Blunt!'

'Yes,' said Miss Blunt, standing there.

'But I just saw you crammed up the flue!'

'No,' laughed Miss Blunt. 'A robot of myself. A clever facsimile!'

'But, but . . .'

'Don't cry, darling. I'm quite all right. Let me look at myself. Well, so there I *am*! Up the chimney. Like you said. Isn't that funny?'

Miss Blunt walked away, laughing.

'Have a drink, Garrett?'

'I believe I will. That unnerved me. My God, what a place. This *does* deserve tearing down. For a moment there . . .'

Garrett drank.

Another scream. Mr. Steffens, borne upon the shoulders of four white rabbits, was carried down a flight of stairs which magically appeared in the floor. Into a pit went Mr. Steffens, where, bound and tied, he was left to face the advancing razor steel of a great pendulum which now whirled down, down, closer and closer to his outraged body.

'Is that me down there?' said Mr. Steffens, appearing at Garrett's elbow. He bent over the pit. 'How strange, how odd, to see yourself die.'

The pendulum made a final stroke.

'How realistic,' said Mr. Steffens, turning away.

'Another drink, Mr. Garrett?'

'Yes, please.'

'It won't be long. The Dismantlers will be here.'

'Thank God!'

And for a third time, a scream.

'What now?' said Garrett apprehensively.

'It's my turn,' said Miss Drummond. 'Look.'

And a second Miss Drummond, shrieking, was nailed into a coffin and thrust into the raw earth under the floor.

'Why, I remember *that*,' gasped the Investigator of Moral

Climates. 'From the old forbidden books. The Premature Burial. And the others. The Pit, the Pendulum, and the ape, the chimney, the Murders in the Rue Morgue. In a book I burned, yes!'

'Another drink, Garrett. Here, hold your glass steady.'

'My lord, you *have* an imagination, haven't you?'

They stood and watched five others die, one in the mouth of a dragon, the others thrown off into the black tarn, sinking and vanishing.

'Would you like to see what we have planned for you?' asked Stendahl.

'Certainly,' said Garrett. 'What's the difference? We'll blow the whole damn thing up, anyway. You're nasty.'

'Come along then. This way.'

And he led Garrett down into the floor, through numerous passages and down again upon spiral stairs into the earth, into the catacombs.

'What do you want to show me down here?' said Garrett.

'Yourself killed.'

'A duplicate?'

'Yes. And also something else.'

'What?'

'The Amontillado,' said Stendahl, going ahead with a blazing lantern which he held high. Skeletons froze half out of coffin lids. Garrett held his hand to his nose, his face disgusted.

'The what?'

'Haven't you ever heard of the Amontillado?'

'No!'

'Don't you recognize this?' Stendahl pointed to a cell.

'Should I?'

'Or this?' Stendahl produced a trowel from under his cape, smiling.

'What's that thing?'

'Come,' said Stendahl.

They stepped into the cell. In the dark, Stendahl affixed the chains to the half-drunken man.

'For God's sake, what are you doing?' shouted Garrett, rattling about.

'I'm being ironic. Don't interrupt a man in the midst of being ironic, it's not polite. There!'

'You've locked me in chains!'

'So I have.'

'What are you going to do?'

'Leave you here.'

'You're joking.'

'A very good joke.'

'Where's my duplicate? Don't we see him killed?'

'There is no duplicate.'

'But the *others*!'

'The others are dead. The ones you saw killed were the real people. The duplicates, the robots, stood by and watched.'

Garrett said nothing.

'Now you're supposed to say, "For the love of God, Montresor!" ' said Stendahl. 'And I will reply, "Yes, for the love of God." Won't you say it? Come on. *Say* it.'

'You fool.'

'Must I coax you? Say it. Say "For the love of God, Montresor!" '

'I won't, you idiot. Get me out of here.' He was sober now.

'Here. Put this on.' Stendahl tossed in something that belled and rang.

'What is it?'

'A cap and bells. Put it on and I might let you out.'

'Stendahl!'

'Put it on, I said!'

Garrett obeyed. The bells tinkled.

'Don't you have a feeling that this has all happened before?' inquired Stendahl, setting to work with trowel and mortar and brick now.

'What're you doing?'

'Walling you in. Here's one row. Here's another.'

'You're insane!'

'I won't argue that point.'

'You'll be prosecuted for this!'

He tapped a brick and placed it on the wet mortar, humming.

Now there was a thrashing and pounding and a crying out from within the darkening place. The bricks rose higher. 'More thrashing, please,' said Stendahl. 'Let's make it a good show.'

'Let me out, let me out!'

There was one last brick to shove into place. The screaming was continuous.

'Garrett?' called Stendahl softly. Garrett silenced himself. 'Garrett,' said Stendahl, 'do you know why I've done this to you? Because you burned Mr. Poe's books without really reading them. You took other people's advice that they needed burning. Otherwise you'd have realized what I was going to do to you when we came down here a moment ago. Ignorance is fatal, Mr. Garrett.'

Garrett was silent.

'I want this to be perfect,' said Stendahl, holding his lantern up so its light penetrated in upon the slumped figure. 'Jingle your bells softly.' The bells rustled. 'Now, if you'll please say, "For the love of God, Montresor," I might let you free.'

The man's face came up in the light. There was a hesitation. Then grotesquely the man said, 'For the love of God, Montresor.'

'Ah,' said Stendahl, eyes closed. He shoved the last brick into place and mortared it tight. *Requiescat in pace*, dear friend.'

He hastened from the catacomb.

In the seven rooms the sound of a midnight clock brought everything to a halt.

The Red Death appeared.

Stendahl turned for a moment at the door to watch. And then he ran out of the great House, across the moat to where a helicopter waited.

'Ready, Pikes?'

'Ready.'

'There it goes!'

They looked at the great House, smiling. It began to crack down the middle, as with an earthquake, and as Stendahl watched the magnificent sight he heard Pikes reciting behind him in a low, cadenced voice:

' "... my brain reeled as I saw the mighty walls rushing asunder; there was a long tumultuous shouting sound like the voice of a thousand waters, and the deep and dank tarn at my feet closed sullenly and silently over the fragments of the House of Usher." '

The helicopter rose over the steaming lake and flew into the west.

THE LAST NIGHT OF THE WORLD

'What would you do if you knew that this was the last night of the world?'

'What would I do? You mean seriously?'

'Yes, seriously.'

'I don't know. I hadn't thought.'

He poured some coffee. In the background the two girls were playing blocks on the parlour rug in the light of the green hurricane lamps. There was an easy, clean aroma of the brewed coffee in the evening air.

'Well, better start thinking about it,' he said.

'You don't mean it!'

He nodded.

'A war?'

He shook his head.

'Not the hydrogen or atom bomb?'

'No.'

'Or germ warfare?'

'None of those at all,' he said, stirring his coffee slowly. 'But just, let's say, the closing of a book.'

'I don't think I understand.'

'No, nor do I, really; it's just a feeling. Sometimes it frightens me, sometimes I'm not frightened at all but at peace.' He glanced in at the girls and their yellow hair shining in the lamplight. 'I didn't say anything to you. It first happened about four nights ago.'

'What?'

'A dream I had. I dreamed that it was all going to be over, and a voice said it was; not any kind of voice I can remember, but a voice anyway, and it said things would stop here on Earth. I didn't think too much about it the next day, but then I went to the office and caught Stan Willis looking out the window in the middle of the afternoon, and I said a penny for your thoughts,

Stan, and he said, I had a dream last night, and before he even told me the dream I knew what it was. I could have told him, but he told me and I listened to him.'

'It was the same dream?'

'The same. I told Stan I had dreamed it too. He didn't seem surprised. He relaxed, in fact. Then we started walking through the office, for the hell of it. It wasn't planned. We didn't say, "Let's walk around." We just walked on our own, and everywhere we saw people looking at their desks or their hands or out windows. I talked to a few. So did Stan.'

'And they all had dreamed?'

'All of them. The same dream, with no difference.'

'Do you believe in it?'

'Yes. I've never been more certain.'

'And when will it stop? The world, I mean.'

'Sometime during the night for us, and then as the night goes on around the world, that'll go too. It'll take twenty-four hours for it all to go.'

They sat awhile not touching their coffee. Then they lifted it slowly and drank, looking at each other.

'Do we deserve this?' she said.

'It's not a matter of deserving; it's just that things didn't work out. I notice you didn't even argue about this. Why not?'

'I guess I've a reason,' she said.

'The same one everyone at the office had?'

She nodded slowly. 'I didn't want to say anything. It happened last night. And the women on the block talked about it, among themselves, today. They dreamed. I thought it was only a coincidence.' She picked up the evening paper. 'There's nothing in the paper about it.'

'Everyone knows, so there's no need.'

He sat back in his chair, watching her. 'Are you afraid?'

'No. I always thought I would be, but I'm not.'

'Where's that spirit called self-preservation they talk so much about?'

'I don't know. You don't get too excited when you feel things are logical. This is logical. Nothing else but this could have happened from the way we've lived.'

'We haven't been too bad, have we?'

'No, nor enormously good. I suppose that's the trouble – we haven't been very much of anything except us, while a big part of the world was busy being lots of quite awful things.'

The girls were laughing in the parlour.

'I always thought people would be screaming in the streets at a time like this.'

'I guess not. You don't scream about the real thing.'

'Do you know, I won't miss anything but you and the girls. I never liked cities or my work or anything except you three. I won't miss a thing except perhaps the change in the weather, and a glass of ice water when it's hot, and I might miss sleeping. How can we sit here and talk this way?'

'Because there's nothing else to do.'

'That's it, of course; for if there were, we'd be doing it. I suppose this is the first time in the history of the world that everyone has known just what they were going to do during the night.'

'I wonder what everyone else will do now, this evening, for the next few hours.'

'Go to a show, listen to the radio, watch television, play cards, put the children to bed, go to bed themselves, like always.'

'In a way that's something to be proud of – like always.'

They sat a moment and then he poured himself another coffee. 'Why do you suppose it's tonight?'

'Because.'

'Why not some other night in the last century, or five centuries ago, or ten?'

'Maybe it's because it was never 19th October, 1969, ever before in history, and now it is and that's it; because this date means more than any other date ever meant; because it's the year when things are as they are all over the world and that's why it's the end.'

'There are bombers on their schedules both ways across the ocean tonight that'll never see land.'

'That's part of the reason why.'

'Well,' he said, getting up, 'what shall it be? Wash the dishes?'

They washed the dishes and stacked them away with special neatness. At eight-thirty the girls were put to bed and kissed good night and the little lights by their beds turned on and the door left open just a trifle.

'I wonder,' said the husband, coming from the bedroom and glancing back, standing there with his pipe for a moment.

'What?'

'If the door will be shut all the way, or if it'll be left just a little ajar so some light comes in.'

'I wonder if the children know.'

'No, of course not.'

They sat and read the papers and talked and listened to some radio music and then sat together by the fireplace watching the charcoal embers as the clock struck ten-thirty and eleven and eleven-thirty. They thought of all the other people in the world who had spent their evening, each in his own special way.

'Well,' he said at last.

He kissed his wife for a long time.

'We've been good for each other, anyway.'

'Do you want to cry?' he asked.

'I don't think so.'

They moved through the house and turned out the lights and went into the bedroom and stood in the night cool darkness undressing and pushing back the covers. 'The sheets are so clean and nice.'

'I'm tired.'

'We're *all* tired.'

They got into bed and lay back.

'Just a moment,' she said.

He heard her get out of bed and go into the kitchen. A moment later, she returned. 'I left the water running in the sink,' she said.

Something about this was so very funny that he had to laugh.

She laughed with him, knowing what it was that she had done that was funny. They stopped laughing at last and lay in their cool night bed, their hands clasped, their heads together.

'Good night,' he said, after a moment.

'Good night,' she said.

THE ROCKET

Many nights Fiorello Bodoni would awaken to hear the rockets sighing in the dark sky. He would tiptoe from bed, certain that his kind wife was dreaming, to let himself out into the night air. For a few moments he would be free of the smells of old food in the small house by the river. For a silent moment he would let his heart soar alone into space, following the rockets.

Now, this very night, he stood half naked in the darkness, watching the fire fountains murmuring in the air. The rockets on their long wild way to Mars and Saturn and Venus!

'Well, well, Bodoni.'

Bodoni started.

On a milk crate, by the silent river, sat an old man who also watched the rockets through the midnight hush.

'Oh, it's you, Bramante!'

'Do you come out every night, Bodoni?'

'Only for the air.'

'So? I prefer the rockets myself,' said old Bramante. 'I was a boy when they started. Eighty years ago, and I've never been on one yet.'

'I will ride up in one someday,' said Bodoni.

'Fool!' cried Bramante. 'You'll never go. This is a rich man's world.' He shook his grey head, remembering. 'When I was young they wrote it in fiery letters: THE WORLD OF THE FUTURE! Science, Comfort and New Things for All! Ha! Eighty years. The Future becomes Now! Do we fly rockets? No! We live in shacks like our ancestors before us.'

'Perhaps my *sons*—' said Bodoni.

'No, nor *their* sons!' the old man shouted. 'It's the rich who have dreams and rockets!'

Bodoni hesitated. 'Old man, I've saved three thousand dollars. It took me six years to save it. For my business, to invest in machinery. But every night for a month now I've been awake. I hear the rockets. I think. And tonight I've made up my mind. One of us will fly to Mars!' His eyes were shining and dark.

'Idiot,' snapped Bramante. 'How will you choose? Who will go? If you go, your wife will hate you, for you will be just a bit nearer God, in space. When you tell your amazing trip to her, over the years, won't bitterness gnaw at her?'

'No, no!'

'Yes! And your children? Will their lives be filled with the memory of Papa, who flew to Mars while they stayed here? What a senseless task you will set your boys. They will think of the rocket all their lives. They will lie awake. They will be sick with wanting it. Just as you are sick now. They will want to die if they cannot go. Don't set that goal, I warn you. Let them be content with being poor. Turn their eyes down to their hands and to your junk yard, not up to the stars.'

'But—'

'Suppose your wife went? How would you feel, knowing she had *seen* and you had not? She would become holy. You would think of throwing her in the river. No, Bodoni, buy a new wrecking machine, which you need, and pull your dreams apart with it, and smash them to pieces.'

The old man subsided, gazing at the river in which, drowned, images of rockets burned down the sky.

'Good night,' said Bodoni.

'Sleep well,' said the other.

When the toast jumped from its silver box, Bodoni almost screamed. The night had been sleepless. Among his nervous children, beside his mountainous wife, Bodoni had twisted and stared at nothing. Bramante was right. Better to invest the money. Why save it when only one of the family could ride the rocket, while the others remained to melt in frustration?

'Fiorello, eat your toast,' said his wife, Maria.

'My throat is shrivelled,' said Bodoni.

The children rushed in, the three boys fighting over a toy rocket, the two girls carrying dolls which duplicated the inhabi-

tants of Mars, Venus, and Neptune, green mannequins with
three yellow eyes and twelve fingers.

'I saw the Venus rocket!' cried Paolo.

'It took off, *whoosh*!' hissed Antonello.

'Children!' shouted Bodoni, hands on his ears.

They stared at him. He seldom shouted.

Bodoni arose. 'Listen, all of you,' he said. 'I have enough
money to take one of us on the Mars rocket.'

Everyone yelled.

'You understand?' he asked. 'Only *one* of us. Who?'

'Me, me, me!' cried the children.

'You,' said Maria.

'You,' said Bodoni to her.

They all fell silent.

The children reconsidered. 'Let Lorenzo go – he's
oldest.'

'Let Miriamne go – she's a girl!'

'Think what you would see,' said Bodoni's wife to him. But
her eyes were strange. Her voice shook. 'The meteors, like fish.
The universe. The Moon. Someone should go who could tell it
well on returning. You have a way with words.'

'Nonsense. So have you,' he objected.

Everyone trembled.

'Here,' said Bodoni unhappily. From a broom he broke
straws of various lengths. 'The short straw wins.' He held out
his tight fist. 'Choose.'

Solemnly each took his turn.

'Long straw.'

'Long straw.'

Another.

'Long straw.'

The children finished. The room was quiet.

Two straws remained. Bodoni felt his heart ache in him.
'Now,' he whispered. 'Maria.'

She drew.

'The short straw,' she said.

'Ah,' sighed Lorenzo, half happy, half sad. 'Mama goes to
Mars.'

Bodoni tried to smile. 'Congratulations. I will buy your ticket today.'

'Wait, Fiorello—'

'You can leave next week,' he murmured.

She saw the sad eyes of her children upon her, with the smiles beneath their straight, large noses. She returned the straw slowly to her husband. 'I cannot go to Mars.'

'But why not?'

'I will be busy with another child.'

'What!'

She would not look at him. 'It wouldn't do for me to travel in my condition.'

He took her elbow. 'Is this the truth?'

'Draw again. Start over.'

'Why didn't you tell me before?' he said incredulously.

'I didn't remember.'

'Maria, Maria,' he whispered, patting her face. He turned to the children. 'Draw again.'

Paolo immediately drew the short straw.

'I go to Mars!' He danced wildly. 'Thank you, Father!'

The other children edged away. 'That's swell, Paolo.'

Paolo stopped smiling to examine his parents and his brothers and sisters. 'I *can* go, can't I?' he asked uncertainly.

'Yes.'

'And you'll *like* me when I come back?'

'Of course.'

Paolo studied the precious broomstraw on his trembling hand and shook his head. He threw it away. 'I forgot. School starts. I can't go. Draw again.'

But none would draw. A full sadness lay on them.

'None of us will go,' said Lorenzo.

'That's best,' said Maria.

'Bramante was right,' said Bodoni.

With his breakfast curdled within him, Fiorello Bodoni worked in his junk yard, ripping metal, melting it, pouring out usable ingots. His equipment flaked apart; competition had kept him on the insane edge of poverty for twenty years. It was a very bad morning.

In the afternoon a man entered the junk yard and called up to Bodoni on his wrecking machine. 'Hey, Bodoni, I got some metal for you!'

'What is it, Mr. Mathews?' asked Bodoni, listlessly.

'A rocket ship. What's wrong? Don't you want it?'

'Yes, yes!' He seized the man's arm, and stopped, bewildered.

'Of course,' said Mathews, 'it's only a mockup. *You* know. When they plan a rocket they build a full-scale model first, of aluminium. You might make a small profit boiling her down. Let you have her for two thousand—'

Bodoni dropped his hand. 'I haven't the money.'

'Sorry. Thought I'd help you. Last time we talked you said how everyone outbid you on junk. Thought I'd slip this to you on the q.t. Well—'

'I need new equipment. I saved money for that.'

'I understand.'

'If I bought your rocket, I wouldn't even be able to melt it down. My aluminium furnace broke down last week—'

'Sure.'

'I couldn't possibly use the rocket if I bought it from you.'

'I know.'

Bodoni blinked and shut his eyes. He opened them and looked at Mr. Mathews. 'But I am a great fool. I will take my money from the bank and give it to you.'

'But if you can't melt the rocket down—'

'Deliver it,' said Bodoni.

'All right, if you say so. Tonight?'

'Tonight,' said Bodoni, 'would be fine. Yes, I would like to have a rocket ship tonight.'

There was a moon. The rocket was white and big in the junk yard. It held the whiteness of the moon and the blueness of the stars. Bodoni looked at it and loved all of it. He wanted to pet it and lie against it, pressing it with his cheek, telling it all the secret wants of his heart.

He stared up at it. 'You are all mine,' he said. 'Even if you never move or spit fire, and just sit there and rust for fifty years, you are mine.'

The rocket smelled of time and distance. It was like walking into a clock. It was finished with Swiss delicacy. One might wear it on one's watch fob.'

'I might even sleep here tonight,' Bodoni whispered excitedly.

He sat in the pilot's seat.

He touched a lever.

He hummed in his shut mouth, his eyes closed.

The humming grew louder, louder, higher, higher, wilder, stranger, more exhilarating, trembling in him and leaning him forward and pulling him and the ship in a roaring silence and in a kind of metal screaming, while his fists flew over the controls, and his shut eyes quivered, and the sound grew and grew until it was a fire, a strength, a lifting and a pushing of power that threatened to tear him in half. He gasped. He hummed again and again, and did not stop, for it could not be stopped, it could only go on, his eyes tighter, his heart furious. 'Taking off!' he screamed. *The jolting concussion! The thunder!* 'The Moon!' he cried, eyes blind, tight. 'The meteors!' *The silent rush in volcanic light.* 'Mars. Oh, God, Mars! Mars!'

He fell back, exhausted and panting. His shaking hands came loose of the controls and his head tilted back wildly. He sat for a long time, breathing out and in, his heart slowing.

Slowly, slowly, he opened his eyes.

The junk yard was still there.

He sat motionless. He looked at the heaped piles of metal for a minute, his eyes never leaving them. Then, leaping up, he kicked the levers. 'Take off, damn you!'

The ship was silent.

'I'll show you!' he cried.

Out in the night air, stumbling, he started the fierce motor of his terrible wrecking machine and advanced upon the rocket. He manoeuvred the massive weights into the moonlit sky. He readied his trembling hands to plunge the weights, to smash, to rip apart this insolently false dream, this silly thing for which he had paid his money, which would not move, which would not do his bidding. 'I'll teach you!' he shouted

But his hand stayed.

The silver rocket lay in the light of the moon. And beyond the rocket stood the yellow lights of his home, a block away, burning warmly. He heard the family radio playing some distant music. He sat for half an hour considering the rocket and the house lights, and his eyes narrowed and grew wide. He stepped down from the wrecking machine and began to walk, and as he walked he began to laugh, and when he reached the back door of his house he took a deep breath and called, 'Maria, Maria, start packing. We're going to Mars!'

'Oh!'

'Ah!'

'I can't *believe* it!'

'You will, you will.'

The children balanced in the windy yard, under the glowing rocket, not touching it yet. They started to cry.

Maria looked at her husband. 'What have you done?' she said. 'Taken our money for this? It will never fly.'

'It will fly,' he said, looking at it.

'Rocket ships cost millions. Have you millions?'

'It will fly,' he repeated steadily. 'Now, go to the house, all of you. I have phone calls to make, work to do. Tomorrow we leave! Tell no one, understand? It is a secret.'

The children edged off from the rocket, stumbling. He saw their small, feverish faces in the house windows, far away.

Maria had not moved. 'You have ruined us,' she said. 'Our money used for this — this thing. When it should have been spent on equipment.'

'You will see,' he said.

Without a word she turned away.

'God help me,' he whispered, and started to work.

Through the midnight hours trucks arrived, packages were delivered, and Bodoni, smiling, exhausted his bank account.

With blow-torch and metal stripping he assaulted the rocket; added, took away, worked fiery magics and secrets upon it. He bolted nine ancient automobile motors into the rocket's empty engine room. Then he welded the engine room shut, so none could see his hidden labour.

At dawn he entered the kitchen. 'Maria,' he said, 'I'm ready for breakfast.'

She would not speak to him.

At sunset he called to the children. 'We're ready! Come on!' The house was silent.

'I've locked them in the closet,' said Maria.

'What do you mean?' he demanded.

'You'll be killed in that rocket,' she said. 'What kind of rocket can you buy for two thousand dollars? A bad one!'

'Listen to me, Maria.'

'It will blow up. Anyway, you are no pilot.'

'Nevertheless, I can fly *this* ship. I have fixed it.'

'You have gone mad,' she said.

'Where is the key to the closet?'

'I have it here.'

He put out his hand. 'Give it to me.'

She handed it to him. 'You will kill them.'

'No, no.'

'Yes, you will. I *feel* it.'

He stood before her. 'You won't come along?'

'I'll stay here,' she said.

'You will understand; you will see then,' he said, and smiled. He unlocked the closet. 'Come, children. Follow your father.'

'Good-bye, good-bye, Mama!'

She stayed in the kitchen window, looking out at them very straight and silent.

At the door of the rocket the father said, 'Children, we will be gone a week. You must come back to school, and I to my business.' He took each of their hands in turn, 'Listen. This rocket is very old and will fly only one more journey. It will not fly again. This will be the one trip of your life. Keep your eyes wide.'

'Yes, Papa.'

'Listen, keep your ears clean. Smell the smells of a rocket. *Feel. Remember.* So when you return you will talk of it all the rest of your lives.'

'Yes, Papa.'

The ship was quiet as a stopped clock. The airlock hissed shut behind them. He strapped them all, like tiny mummies, into rubber hammocks. 'Ready?' he called.

'Ready!' all replied.

'Take-off!' He jerked ten switches. The rocket thundered and leaped. The children danced in their hammocks screaming.

'Here comes the Moon!'

The Moon dreamed by. Meteors broke into fireworks. Time flowed away in a serpentine of gas. The children shouted. Released from their hammocks, hours later, they peered from the ports. 'There's Earth!' 'There's Mars!'

The rocket dropped pink petals of fire while the hour dials spun; the child eyes dropped shut. At last they hung like drunken moths in their cocoon hammocks.

'Good,' whispered Bodoni, alone.

He tiptoed from the control room to stand for a long moment, fearful, at the airlock door.

He pressed a button. The airlock door swung wide. He stepped out. Into space? Into inky tides of meteor and gaseous torch? Into swift mileages and infinite dimensions?

No. Bodoni smiled.

All about the quivering rocket lay the junk yard.

Rusting, unchanged, there stood the padlocked junk yard gate, the little silent house by the river, the kitchen window lighted, and the river going down to the same sea. And in the centre of the junk yard, manufacturing a magic dream, lay the quivering, purring rocket. Shaking and roaring, bouncing the netted children like flies in a web.

Maria stood in the kitchen window.

He waved to her and smiled.

He could not see if she waved or not. A small wave, perhaps. A small smile.

The sun was rising.

Bodoni withdrew hastily into the rocket. Silence. All still slept. He breathed easily. Tying himself into a hammock, he closed his eyes. To himself he prayed, Oh, let nothing happen to the illusion in the next six days. Let all of space come and go, and red Mars come up under our ship, and the moons of Mars, and let there be no flaws in the colour film. Let there be three dimensions; let nothing go wrong with the hidden mirrors and screens that mould the fine illusion. Let time pass without crisis.

He awoke.

Red Mars floated near the rocket.

'Papa!' The children thrashed to be free.

Bodoni looked and saw red Mars and it was good and there was no flaw in it and he was very happy.

At sunset on the seventh day the rocket stopped shuddering.

'We are home,' said Bodoni.

They walked across the junk yard from the open door of the rocket, their blood singing, their faces glowing.

'I have ham and eggs for all of you,' said Maria, at the kitchen door.

'Mama, Mama, you should have come, to see it, to see Mars, Mama, and meteors, and everything!'

'Yes,' she said.

At bedtime the children gathered before Bodoni. 'We want to thank you, Papa.'

'It was nothing.'

'We will remember it for always, Papa. We will never forget.'

Very late in the night Bodoni opened his eyes. He sensed that his wife was lying beside him, watching him. She did not move for a very long time, and then suddenly she kissed his cheeks and his forehead. 'What's this?' he cried.

'You're the best father in the world,' she whispered.

'Why?'

'Now I see,' she said. 'I understand.'

She lay back and closed her eyes, holding his hand. 'Is it a very lovely journey?' she asked.

'Yes,' he said.

'Perhaps,' she said, 'perhaps, some night, you might take me on just a little trip, do you think?'

'Just a little one, perhaps,' he said.

'Thank you,' she said. 'Good night.'

'Good night,' said Fiorello Bodoni.

NO PARTICULAR NIGHT OR MORNING

He had smoked a packet of cigarettes in two hours.

'How far out in space are we?'

'A billion miles.'

'A billion miles from where?' said Hitchcock.

'It all depends,' said Clemens, not smoking at all. 'A billion miles from home, you might say.'

'Then *say* it.'

'Home. Earth. New York, Chicago. Wherever you were from.'

'I don't even remember,' said Hitchcock. 'I don't even believe there is an Earth now, do you?'

'Yes,' said Clemens. 'I dreamt about it this morning.'

'There is no morning in space.'

'During the night then.'

'It's always night,' said Hitchcock quietly. 'Which night do you mean?'

'Shut up,' said Clemens irritably. 'Let me finish.'

Hitchcock lit another cigarette. His hand did not shake, but it looked as if, inside the sunburned flesh, it might be tremoring all to itself, a small tremor in each hand and a large invisible tremor in his body. The two men sat on the observation corridor floor, looking out at the stars. Clemens's eyes flashed, but Hitchcock's eyes focused on nothing; they were blank and puzzled.

'I woke up at 0500 hours myself,' said Hitchcock, as if he were talking to his right hand. 'And I heard myself screaming, "Where am I? Where am I?" And the answer was "Nowhere!" And I said, "Where've I been?" And I said, "Earth!" "What's Earth?" I wondered. "Where I was born," I said. But it was nothing and worse than nothing. I don't believe in anything I can't see or hear or touch. I can't see Earth, so why should I believe in it? It's safer this way, not to believe.'

'There's Earth.' Clemens pointed, smiling. 'That point of light there.'

'That's not Earth; that's our sun. You can't see Earth from here.'

'I can see it. I have a good memory.'

'It's not the *same*, you fool,' said Hitchcock suddenly. There was a touch of anger in his voice. 'I mean *see* it. I've always been that way. When I'm in Boston, New York is dead. When I'm in New York, Boston is dead. When I don't see a man for a day, he's dead. When he comes walking down the street, my God, it's a resurrection. I do a dance, almost, I'm so glad to see him. I used to, anyway. I don't dance any more. I just look. And when the man walks off, he's dead again.'

Clemens laughed. 'It's simply that your mind works on a primitive level. You can't hold to things. You've got no imagination, Hitchcock old man. You've got to learn to hold on.'

'Why should I hold on to things I can't use?' said Hitchcock, his eyes wide, still staring into space. 'I'm practical. If Earth isn't here for me to walk on, you want me to walk on a memory? That *hurts*. Memories, as my father once said, are porcupines. To hell with them! Stay away from them. They make you unhappy. They ruin your work. They make you cry.'

'I'm walking on Earth right now,' said Clemens, squinting to himself, blowing smoke.

'You're kicking porcupines. Later in the day you won't be able to eat lunch, and you'll wonder why,' said Hitchcock in a dead voice. 'And it'll be because you've got a footful of quills aching in you. To hell with it! If I can't drink it, pinch it, punch it, or lie on it, then I say drop it in the sun. I'm dead to Earth. It's dead to me. There's no one in New York weeping for me tonight. Shove New York. There isn't any season here; winter and summer are gone. So is spring, and autumn. It isn't any particular night or morning, it's space and space. The only thing right now is you and me and this rocket ship. And the only thing I'm positive of is *me*. That's all of it.'

Clemens ignored this. 'I'm putting a nickel in the phone slot right now,' he said, pantomiming it with a slow smile. 'And calling my girl in Evanston. Hello, Barbara!'

The rocket sailed on through space.

The lunch bell rang at 1305 hours. The men ran by on soft rubber sneakers and sat at the cushioned tables.

Clemens wasn't hungry.

'See, what did I tell you!' said Hitchcock. 'You and your damned porcupines! Leave them alone, like I told you. Look at me, shovelling away food.' He said this with a mechanical, slow, and unhumorous voice. 'Watch me.' He put a big piece of pie in his mouth and felt it with his tongue. He looked at the pie on his plate as if to see the texture. He moved it with his fork. He felt the fork handle. He mashed the lemon filling and watched it jet up between the tines. Then he touched a bottle of milk all over and poured out half a quart into a glass, listening to it. He looked at the milk as if to make it whiter. He drank the milk so swiftly that he couldn't have tasted it. He had eaten his entire lunch in a few minutes, cramming it in feverishly, and now he looked around for more, but it was gone. He gazed out the window of the rocket, blankly. 'Those aren't real, either,' he said.

'What?' asked Clemens.

'The stars. Who's ever touched one? I can see them, sure, but what's the use of seeing a thing that's a million or a billion miles away? Anything that far off isn't worth bothering with.'

'Why did you come on this trip?' asked Clemens suddenly.

Hitchcock peered into his amazingly empty milk glass and clenched it tight, then relaxed his hand and clenched it again. I don't know.' He ran his tongue on the glass rim. 'I just had to, is all. How do you know why you do anything in this life?'

'You liked the idea of space travel? Going places?'

'I don't know. Yes. No. It wasn't going places. It was being *between*.' Hitchcock for the first time tried to focus his eyes upon something, but it was so nebulous and far off that his eyes couldn't make the adjustment, though he worked his face and hands. 'Mostly it was space. So much space. I liked the idea of nothing on top, nothing on the bottom, and a lot of nothing in between, and me in the middle of the nothing.'

'I never heard it put that way before.'

'*I* just put it that way; I hope you listened.'

Hitchcock took out his cigarettes and lit up and began to suck and blow the smoke, again and again.

Clemens said, 'What sort of childhood did you have, Hitchcock?'

'I was never young. Whoever I was then is dead. That's more of your quills. I don't want a hide full, thanks. I've always figured it that you die each day, and each day is a box, you see, all numbered and neat; but never go back and lift the lids, because you've died a couple of thousand times in your life, and that's a lot of corpses, each dead a different way, each with a worse expression. Each of those days is a different you, somebody you don't know or understand or want to understand.'

'You're cutting yourself off, that way.'

'Why should I have anything to do with that younger Hitchcock? He was a fool, and he was yanked around and he was glad when his mother died, because she was the same. Should I go back and see his face on that day and gloat over it? He was a fool.'

'We're all fools,' said Clemens, 'all the time. It's just we're a different kind each day. We think, I'm not a fool today. I've learned my lesson. I was a fool yesterday but not this morning. Then tomorrow we find out that, yes, we were a fool today too. I think the only way we can grow and get on in this world is to accept the fact we're not perfect and live accordingly.'

'I don't want to remember imperfect things,' said Hitchcock. 'I can't shake hands with that younger Hitchcock, can I? Where is he? Can you find him for me? He's dead, so to hell with him! I won't shape what I do tomorrow by some lousy thing I did yesterday.'

'You've got it wrong.'

'Let me have it then.' Hitchcock sat, finished with his meal, looking out of the port. The other men glanced at him.

'Do meteors exist?' asked Hitchcock.

'You know damn well they do.'

'In our radar machines – yes, as streaks of light in space. No, I don't believe in anything that doesn't exist and act in my presence. Sometimes' – he nodded at the men finishing their food – 'sometimes I don't believe in anyone or anything but me.' He sat up. 'Is there an upstairs to this ship?'

'Yes.'

'I've got to see it immediately.'

'Don't get excited.'

'You wait here; I'll be right back.' Hitchcock walked out swiftly. The other men sat nibbling their food slowly. A moment passed. One of the men raised his head. 'How long's this been going on? I mean Hitchcock.'

'Just today.'

'He acted funny the other day too.'

'Yes, but it's worse today.'

'Has anyone told the psychiatrist?'

'We thought he'd come out of it. Everyone has a little touch of space the first time out. I've had it. You get wildly philosophical, then frightened. You break into a sweat, then you doubt your parentage, you don't believe in Earth, you get drunk, wake up with a hangover, and that's it.'

'But Hitchcock don't get drunk,' said someone. 'I wish he would.'

'How'd he ever get past the examining board?'

'How'd we all get past? They need men. Space scares the hell out of most people. So the board lets a lot of borderlines through.'

'That man isn't a borderline,' said someone. 'He's a fall-off-a-cliff-and-no-bottom-to-hit.'

They waited for five minutes. Hitchcock didn't come back.

Clemens finally got up and went out and climbed the circular stair to the flight deck above. Hitchcock was there, touching the wall tenderly.

'It's here,' he said.

'Of course it is.'

'I was afraid it might not be.' Hitchcock peered at Clemens. 'And you're alive.'

'I have been for a long time.'

'No,' said Hitchcock. 'No, just *now* this *instant*, while you're here with me, you're alive. A moment ago you weren't anything.'

'I was to me,' said the other.

'That's not important. You weren't here with me,' said Hitchcock. 'Only that's important. Is the crew down below?'

'Yes.'

'Can you prove it?'

'Look, Hitchcock, you'd better see Dr. Edwards. I think you need a little servicing.'

'No, I'm all right. Who's the doctor, anyway? Can you prove he's on this ship?'

'I can. All I have to do is call him.'

'No. I mean, standing here, in this instant, you can't prove he's here, can you?'

'Not without moving, I can't.'

'You see. You have no mental evidence. That's what I want, a mental evidence I can *feel*. I don't want physical evidence, proof you have to go out and drag in. I want evidence that you can carry in your mind and always touch and smell and feel. But there's no way to do that. In order to believe in a thing you've got to carry it with you. You can't carry the Earth, or a man, in your pocket. I want a way to do that, carry things with me always, so I can believe in them. How clumsy to have to go to all the trouble of going out and bringing in something terribly physical to prove something. I hate physical things because they can be left behind and become impossible to believe in then.'

'Those are the rules of the game.'

'I want to change them. Wouldn't it be fine if we could *prove* things with our mind, and know for certain that things are always in their place. I'd like to know what a place is *like* when I'm *not there*. I'd like to be *sure*.'

'That's not possible.'

'You know,' said Hitchcock, 'I first got the idea of coming

out into space about five years ago. About the time I lost my job. Did you know I wanted to be a writer? Oh yes, one of those men who always talk about writing but rarely write. And too much temper. So I lost my good job and left the editorial business and couldn't get another job and went on down hill. Then my wife died. You see, nothing stays where you put it — you can't trust material things. I had to put my boy in an aunt's trust, and things got worse; then one day I had a story published with my name on it, but it wasn't me.

'I don't get you.'

Hitchcock's face was pale and sweating.

'I can only say that I looked at the page with my name under the title. By Joseph Hitchcock. But it was some other man. There was no way to *prove* — actually *prove*, *really* prove — that that man was me. The story was familiar — I knew I had written it — but that name on the paper still was not me. It was a symbol, a name. It was alien. And then I realized that even if I did become successful at writing, it would never mean a thing to me, because I couldn't identify myself with that name. It would be soot and ashes. So I didn't write any more. I was never sure, anyway, that the stories I had in my desk a few days later were mine, though I remembered typing them. There was always that gap of proof. That gap between doing and having done. What is done is dead and is not proof, for it is not an action. Only actions are important. And pieces of paper were remains of actions done and over and now unseen. The proof of doing was over and done. Nothing but memory remained, and I didn't trust my memory. Could I actually *prove* I'd written these stories? No. Can *any* author? I mean *proof*. I mean action as proof. No. Not really. Not unless someone sits in the room while you type, and then maybe you're doing it from memory. And once a thing is accomplished there is no proof, only memory. So then I began to find gaps between everything. I doubted I was married or had a child or ever had a job in my life. I doubted that I had been born in Illinois and had a drunken father and swinish mother. I couldn't prove anything. Oh yes, people could say, "You are thus and so and such and such," but that was nothing.'

'You should get your mind off stuff like that,' said Clemens.

'I can't. All the gaps and spaces. And that's how I got to thinking about the stars. I thought how I'd like to be in a rocket ship, in space, in nothing, in *nothing*, going on into nothing, with just a thin something, a thin eggshell of metal holding me, going on away from all the somethings with gaps in them that couldn't prove themselves. I knew then that the only happiness for me was space. When I get to Aldebaran II I'll sign up to return on the five-year journey to Earth and so go back and forth like a shuttlecock all the rest of my life.'

'Have you talked about this to the psychiatrist?'

'So he could try to mortar up the gaps for me, fill in the gulfs with noise and warm water and words and hands touching me, and all that? No, thanks.' Hitchcock stopped. 'I'm getting worse, aren't I? I thought so. This morning when I woke up I thought, I'm getting worse. Or is it better?' He paused again and cocked an eye at Clemens. Are you there? Are you *really* there? Go on, prove it.'

Clemens slapped him on the arm, hard.

'Yes,' said Hitchcock, rubbing his arm, looking at it very thoroughly, wonderingly, massaging it. 'You were there. For a brief fraction of an instant. But I wonder if you are – now.'

'See you later,' said Clemens. He was on his way to find the doctor. He walked away.

A bell rang. Two bells, three bells rang. The ship rocked as if a hand had slapped it. There was a sucking sound, the sound of a vacuum cleaner turned on. Clemens heard the screams and felt the air thin. The air hissed away about his ears. Suddenly there was nothing in his nose or lungs. He stumbled and then the hissing stopped.

He heard someone cry, 'A meteor.' Another said, 'It's patched!' And this was true. The ship's emergency spider, running over the outside of the hull, had slapped a hot patch on the hole in the metal and welded it tight.

Someone was talking and talking and then beginning to shout at a distance. Clemens ran along the corridor through the freshening, thickening air. As he turned in at a bulkhead he saw the hole in the steel wall, freshly sealed; he saw the meteor fragments lying about the room like bits of a toy. He saw the captain and the members of the crew and a man lying on the floor. It was Hitchcock. His eyes were closed and he was crying. 'It tried to kill me,' he said, over and over. 'It tried to kill me.' They got him on his feet. 'It can't do that,' said Hitchcock. 'That's not how it should be. Things like that can't happen, can they? It came in after me. Why did it do that?'

'All right, all right, Hitchcock,' said the captain.

The doctor was bandaging a small cut on Hitchcock's arm, Hitchcock looked up, his face pale, and saw Clemens there looking at him. 'It tried to *kill* me,' he said.

'I know,' said Clemens.

Seventeen hours passed. The ship moved on in space.

Clemens stepped through a bulkhead and waited. The psychiatrist and the captain were there. Hitchcock sat on the floor with his legs drawn up to his chest, arms wrapped tight about them.

'Hitchcock,' said the captain.

No answer.

'Hitchcock, listen to me,' said the psychiatrist.

They turned to Clemens. 'You're his friend?'

'Yes.'

'Do you want to help us?'

'If I can.'

'It was that damned meteor,' said the captain. 'This might not have happened if it hadn't been for that.'

'It would've come anyway, sooner or later,' said the doctor. To Clemens: 'You might talk to him.'

Clemens walked quietly over and crouched by Hitchcock and began to shake his arm gently, calling in a low voice, 'Hey there, Hitchcock.'

No reply.

'Hey, it's me. Me, Clemens,' said Clemens. 'Look, I'm here.' He gave the arm a little slap. He massaged the rigid neck, gently, and the back of the bent-down head. He glanced at the psychiatrist, who sighed very softly. The captain shrugged.

'Shock treatment, Doctor?'

The psychiatrist nodded. 'We'll start within the hour.'

Yes, thought Clemens, shock treatment. Play a dozen jazz records for him, wave a bottle of fresh green chlorophyll and dandelions under his nose, put grass under his feet, squirt Chanel on the air, cut his hair, clip his fingernails, bring him a woman, shout, bang and crash at him, fry him with electricity, fill the gap and the gulf, but where's your proof? You can't keep proving to him forever. You can't entertain a baby with rattles and sirens all night every night for the next thirty years. Sometime you've got to stop. When you do that, he's lost again. That is, if he pays any attention to you at all.

'Hitchcock!' he cried, as loud as he could, almost frantically, as if he himself were falling over a cliff. 'It's me. It's your pal! Hey!'

Clemens turned and walked away out of the silent room.

Twelve hours later another alarm bell rang.

After all the running had died down, the captain explained: 'Hitchcock snapped out of it for a minute or so. He was alone. He climbed into a space suit. He opened an airlock. Then he walked out into space – alone.'

Clemens blinked through the immense glass port, where was a blur of stars and distant blackness. 'He's out there now?'

'Yes. A million miles behind us. We'd never find him. First time I knew he was outside the ship was when his helmet radio came in on our control-room beam. I heard him talking to himself.'

'What did he say?'

'Something like "No more space ship now. Never was any. No people. No people in all the universe. Never were any. No planets. No stars." That's what he said. And then he said something about his hands and feet and legs. "No hands," he said. "I haven't any hands any more. Never had any. No feet. Never had any. Can't prove it. No body. Never had any. No lips. No face. No head. Nothing. Only space. Only space. Only the gap." '

The men turned quietly to look from the glass port out into the remote and cold stars.

Space, thought Clemens. The space that Hitchcock loved so well. Space, with nothing on top, nothing on the bottom, a lot of empty nothings between, and Hitchcock falling in the middle of the nothing, on his way to no particular night and no particular morning. ⁙ ⁙ ⁙

THE FOX AND THE FOREST

There were fireworks the very first night, things that you should be afraid of perhaps, for they might remind you of other more horrible things, but these were beautiful, rockets that ascended into the ancient soft air of Mexico and shook the stars apart in blue and white fragments. Everything was good and sweet, the air was that blend of the dead and the living, of the rains and the dusts, of the incense from the church, and the brass smell of the tubas on the bandstand which pulsed out vast rhythms of 'La Paloma'. The church doors were thrown wide and it seemed as if a giant yellow constellation had fallen from the October sky and lay breathing fire upon the church walls; a million candles sent their colour and fumes about. Newer and better fireworks scurried like tight-rope-walking comets across the cool-tiled square, banged against adobe café walls, then rushed on hot wires to bash the high church tower, in which boys' naked feet alone could be seen kicking and re-kicking, clanging and tilting and re-tilting the monster bells into monstrous music. A flaming bull blundered about the plaza chasing laughing men and screaming children.

'The year is 1938,' said William Travis, standing by his wife on the edge of the yelling crowd, smiling. 'A good year.'

The bull rushed upon them. Ducking, the couple ran, with fire balls pelting them, past the music and riot, the church, the band, under the stars, clutching each other, laughing. The bull passed, carried lightly on the shoulders of a charging Mexican, a framework of bamboo and sulphurous gunpowder.

'I've never enjoyed myself so much in my life.' Susan Travis had stopped for her breath.

'It's amazing,' said William.

'It will go on, won't it?'

'All night.'

'No, I mean our trip.'

He frowned and patted his breast pocket. 'I've enough traveller's cheques for a lifetime. Enjoy yourself. Forget it. They'll never find us.'

'Never?'

'Never.'

Now someone was setting off giant crackers, hurling them from the great bell-tolling tower of the church in a sputter of smoke, while the crowd below fell back under the threat and the crackers exploded in wonderful concussions among their dancing feet and flailing bodies. A wondrous smell of frying tortillas hung all about, and in the cafés men sat at tables looking out, mugs of beer in their brown hands.

The bull was dead. The fire was out of the bamboo tubes and he was expended. The labourer lifted the framework from his shoulders. Little boys clustered to touch the magnificent papier-mâché head, the real horns.

'Let's examine the bull,' said William.

As they walked past the café entrance Susan saw the man looking out at them, a white man in a salt-white suit, with a blue tie and blue shirt, and a thin, sunburned face. His hair was blond and straight and his eyes were blue, and he watched them as they walked.

She would never have noticed him if it had not been for the bottles at his immaculate elbow; a fat bottle of crème de menthe, a clear bottle of vermouth, a flagon of cognac, and seven other bottles of assorted liqueurs, and, at his finger tips, ten small half-filled glasses from which, without taking his eyes off the street, he sipped, occasionally squinting, pressing his thin mouth shut upon the savour. In his free hand a thin Havana cigar smoked, and on a chair stood twenty cartons of Turkish cigarettes, six boxes of cigars, and some packaged colognes.

'Bill—' whispered Susan.

'Take it easy,' he said. 'He's nobody.'

'I saw him in the plaza this morning.'

'Don't look back, keep walking. Examine the papier-mâché bull here. That's it, ask questions.'

'Do you think he's from the Searchers?'

'They couldn't follow us!'

'They might!'

'What a nice bull,' said William to the man who owned it.

'He couldn't have followed us back through two hundred years, could he?'

'Watch yourself, for God's sake,' said William.

She swayed. He crushed her elbow tightly, steering her away.

'Don't faint.' He smiled, to make it look good. 'You'll be all right. Let's go right in that café, drink in front of him, so if he *is* what we think he is, he won't suspect.'

'No, I couldn't.'

'We've *got* to. Come on now. And so I said to David, that's ridiculous!' This last in a loud voice as they went up the café steps.

We are here, thought Susan. Who are we? Where are we going? What do we fear? Start at the beginning, she told herself, holding to her sanity, as she felt the adobe floor underfoot.

My name is Ann Kristen; my husband's name is Roger. We were born in the year 2155 A.D. And we lived in a world that was evil. A world that was like a great black ship pulling away from the shore of sanity and civilization, roaring its black horn in the night, taking two billion people with it, whether they wanted to go or not, to death, to fall over the edge of the earth and the sea into radioactive flame and madness.

They walked into the café. The man was staring at them.

A phone rang.

The phone startled Susan. She remembered a phone ringing two hundred years in the future, on that blue April morning in 2155, and herself answering it:

'Ann, this is Rene! Have you heard? I mean about Travel in Time, Incorporated? Trips to Rome in 21 B.C., trips to Napoleon's Waterloo – any time, any place!'

'Rene, you're joking.'

'No. Clinton Smith left this morning for Philadelphia in 1776. Travel in Time, Inc., arranges everything. Costs money.

But, *think* – to actually *see* the burning of Rome, Kubla Khan, Moses and the Red Sea! You've probably got an ad. in your tube mail now.'

She had opened the suction mail tube and there was the metal foil advertisement:

ROME AND THE BORGIAS!
THE WRIGHT BROTHERS AT KITTY HAWK!

Travel in Time, Inc., can costume you, put you in a crowd during the assassination of Lincoln or Caesar! We guarantee to teach you any language you need to move freely in any civilization, in any year, without friction. Latin, Greek, ancient American colloquial. Take your vacation in *Time* as well as Place!

Rene's voice was buzzing on the phone. 'Tom and I leave for 1492 tomorrow. They're arranging for Tom to sail with Columbus. Isn't it amazing!'

'Yes,' murmured Ann, stunned. 'What does the Government say about this Time Machine company?'

'Oh, the police have an eye on it. Afraid people might evade the draft, run off and hide in the Past. Everyone has to leave a security bond behind, his house and belongings, to guarantee return. After all, the war's on.'

'Yes, the war,' murmured Ann. 'The war.'

Standing there, holding the phone, she had thought, here is the chance my husband and I have talked and prayed over for so many years. We don't like this world of 2155. We want to run away from his work at the bomb factory. I from my position with disease-culture units. Perhaps there is a chance for us to escape, to run for centuries into a wild country of years where they will never find and bring us back to burn our books, censor our thoughts, scald our minds with fear, march us, scream at us with radios . . .

They were in Mexico in the year 1938.
She looked at the stained café wall.
Good workers for the Future State were allowed vacations

into the Past to escape fatigue. And so she and her husband had moved back into 1938, a room in New York City, and enjoyed the theatres and the Statue of Liberty, which still stood green in the harbour. And on the third day they had changed their clothes, their names, and had flown off to hide in Mexico!

'It *must* be him,' whispered Susan, looking at the stranger seated at the table. 'Those cigarettes, the cigars, the liquor. They give him away. Remember *our* first night in the Past?'

A month ago, their first night in New York, before their flight, drinking all the strange drinks, savouring and buying odd foods, perfumes, cigarettes of ten dozen rare brands, for they were rare in the Future, where war was everything. So they had made fools of themselves, rushing in and out of stores, salons, tobacconists, going up to their room to get wonderfully ill.

And now here was this stranger doing likewise, doing a thing that only a man from the Future would do who had been starved for liquors and cigarettes for many years.

Susan and William sat and ordered a drink.

The stranger was examining their clothes, their hair, their jewellery – the way they walked and sat.

'Sit easily,' said William under his breath. 'Look as if you've worn this clothing style all your life.'

'We should never have tried to escape.'

'My God!' said William, 'he's coming over. Let me do the talking.'

The stranger bowed before them. There was the faintest tap of heels knocking together. Susan stiffened. That military sound! – unmistakable as that certain ugly rap on your door at midnight.

'Mr. Roger Kristen,' said the stranger, 'you did not pull up your pant legs when you sat down.'

William froze. He looked at his hands lying on either leg, innocently. Susan's heart was beating swiftly.

'You've got the wrong person,' said William quickly. 'My name's not Krisler.'

'Kris*ten*,' corrected the stranger.

'I'm William Travis,' said William. 'And I don't see what my pant legs have to do with you!'

'Sorry.' The stranger pulled up a chair. 'Let us say I thought I knew you because you did *not* pull your trousers up. *Everyone* does. If they don't, the trousers bag quickly. I am a long way from home, Mr. — Travis, and in need of company. My name is Simms.'

'Mr. Simms, we appreciate your loneliness, but we're tired. We're leaving for Acapulco tomorrow.'

'A charming spot. I was just there, looking for some friends of mine. They are somewhere. I shall find them yet. Oh, is the lady a bit sick?'

'Good night, Mr. Simms.'

They started out of the door, William holding Susan's arm firmly. They did not look back when Mr. Simms called, 'Oh, just one other thing.' He paused and then slowly spoke the words: '2155 A.D.'

Susan shut her eyes and felt the earth falter under her. She kept going, into the fiery plaza, seeing nothing.

They locked the door of their hotel room. And then she was crying and they were standing in the dark, and the room tilted under them. Far away firecrackers exploded, and there was laughter in the plaza.

'What a damned, loud nerve,' said William. 'Him sitting there, looking us up and down like animals, smoking his damn cigarettes, drinking his drinks. I should have killed him then!' His voice was nearly hysterical. 'He even had the nerve to use his real name to us. The Chief of the Searchers. And the thing about my pant legs. My God, I should have pulled them up when I sat. It's an automatic gesture of this day and age. When I didn't do it, it set me off from the others; it made *him* think, Here's a man who never wore pants, a man used to breech uniforms and future styles. I could kill myself for giving us away!'

'No, no, it was my walk — these high heels — that did it. Our haircuts — so new, so fresh. Everything about us odd and uneasy.'

He turned on the light. 'He's still testing us. He's not positive of us — not completely. We can't run out on him, then. We can't make him certain. We'll go to Acapulco leisurely.'

'Maybe he *is* sure of us, but is just playing.'

'I wouldn't put it past him. He's got all the time in the world. He can dally here if he wants, and bring us back to the Future sixty seconds after we left it. He might keep us wondering for days, laughing at us.'

Susan sat on the bed, wiping the tears from her face, smelling the old smell of charcoal and incense.

'They won't make a scene, will they?'

'They won't dare. They'll have to get us alone to put us in that Time Machine and send us back.'

'There's a solution then,' she said. 'We'll never be alone; we'll always be in crowds. We'll make a million friends, visit markets, sleep in the Official Palaces in each town, pay the Chief of Police to guard us until we find a way to kill Simms and escape, disguise ourselves in new clothes, perhaps as Mexicans.'

Footsteps sounded outside their locked door.

They turned out the light and undressed in silence. The footsteps went away. A door closed.

Susan stood by the window looking down at the plaza in the darkness. 'So that building there is a church?'

'Yes.'

'I've often wondered what a church looked like. It's been so long since anyone saw one. Can we visit it tomorrow?'

'Of course. Come to bed.'

They lay in the dark room.

Half an hour later their phone rang. She lifted the receiver.

'Hello?'

'The rabbits may hide in the forest,' said a voice, 'but a fox can always find them.'

She replaced the receiver and lay back straight and cold in the bed.

Outside, in the year 1938, a man played three tunes upon a guitar, one following another.

During the night she put her hand out and almost touched the year 2155. She felt her fingers slide over cool spaces of time, as over a corrugated surface, and she heard the insistent thump of marching feet, a million bands playing a million military tunes, and she saw the fifty thousand rows of disease cultures in their aseptic glass tubes, her hand reaching out to them at her work in that huge factory in the Future; the tubes of leprosy, bubonic, typhoid, tuberculosis, and then the great explosion. She saw her hand burned to a wrinkled plum, felt it recoil from a concussion so immense that the world was lifted and let fall and all the buildings broke and people haemorrhaged and lay silent. Great volcanoes, machines, winds, avalanches slid down to silence and she awoke, sobbing, in the bed, in Mexico, many years away. . . .

In the early morning, drugged with the single hour's sleep they had finally been able to obtain, they awoke to the sound of loud automobiles in the street. Susan peered down from the iron balcony at a small crowd of eight people only now emerging, chattering, yelling, from trucks and cars with red lettering on them. A crowd of Mexicans had followed the trucks.

'*Qué pasa?*' Susan called to a little boy.

The boy replied.

Susan turned back to her husband. 'An American motion-picture company, here on location.'

'Sounds interesting.' William was in the shower. 'Let's watch them. I don't think we'd better leave today. We'll try to lull Simms. Watch the films being made. They say the primitive film-making was something. Get our minds off ourselves.'

Ourselves, thought Susan. For a moment, in the bright sun, she had forgotten that somewhere in the hotel, waiting, was a man smoking a thousand cigarettes, it seemed. She saw the eight loud happy Americans below and wanted to call to them: 'Save me, hide me, help me! Colour my hair, my eyes; clothe me in strange clothes. I need your help. I'm from the year 2155!'

But the words stayed in her throat. The functionaries of Travel in Time, Inc., were not foolish. In your brain, before you left on your trip, they placed a psychological bloc. You could tell no one your true time or birthplace, nor could you reveal any of the Future to those in the Past. The Past and the Future must be protected from each other. Only with this psychological bloc were people allowed to travel unguarded through the ages. The Future must be protected from any chance brought about by her people travelling in the Past. Even if she wanted to with all her heart, she could not tell any of those happy people below in the plaza who she was, or what her predicament had become.

'What about breakfast?' said William.

Breakfast was being served in the immense dining-room. Ham and eggs for everyone. The place was full of tourists. The film people entered, all eight of them – six men and two women, giggling, shoving chairs about. And Susan sat near them, feeling the warmth and protection they offered, even when Mr. Simms came down the lobby stairs smoking his Turkish cigarette with great intensity. He nodded at them from a distance, and Susan nodded back, smiling, because he couldn't do anything to them here, in front of eight film people and twenty other tourists.

'Those actors,' said William. 'Perhaps I could hire two of them, say it was a joke, dress them in our clothes, have them drive off in our car, when Simms is in such a spot where he can't see their faces. If two people pretending to be us could lure him off for a few hours, we might make it to the Mexico City. It'd take him years to find us there!'

'Hey!'

A fat man, with liquor on his breath, leaned on their table.

'American tourists!' he cried. 'I'm so sick of seeing Mexicans, I could kiss you!' He shook their hands. 'Come on, eat with us. Misery loves company. I'm Misery, this is Miss Gloom, and Mr. and Mrs. Do-We-Hate-Mexico! We all hate it. But we're here for some preliminary shots for a damn film. The rest of the crew arrives tomorrow. My name's Joe Melton. I'm a director. And if this ain't a hell of a country! Funerals in

the streets, people dying. Come on, move over. Join the party;
cheer us up!'

Susan and William were both laughing.

'Am I funny?' Mr. Melton asked the immediate world.

'Wonderful!' Susan moved over.

Mr. Simms was glaring across the dining-room at them.

She made a face at him.

Mr. Simms advanced among the tables.

'Mr. and Mrs. Travis,' he called. 'I thought we were break-
fasting together alone.'

'Sorry,' said William.

'Sit down pal,' said Mr. Melton. 'Any friend of theirs is a
pal of mine.'

Mr. Simms sat. The film people talked loudly, and while
they talked, Mr Simms said quietly, 'I hope you slept well.'

'Did you?'

'I'm not used to spring mattresses,' replied Mr. Simms wryly.
'But there are compensations. I stayed up half the night trying
new cigarettes and foods. Odd, fascinating. A whole new spec-
trum of sensation, these ancient vices.'

'We don't know what you're talking about,' said Susan.

'Always the play-acting.' Simms laughed. 'It's no use. Nor is
this stratagem of crowds. I'll get you alone soon enough. I'm
immensely patient.'

'Say,' Mr. Melton broke in, his face flushed, 'is this guy
giving you any trouble?'

'It's all right.'

'Say the word and I'll give him the bum's rush.'

Melton turned back to yell at his associates. In the laughter,
Mr. Simms went on: 'Let us come to the point. It took me a
month of tracing you through towns and cities to find you, and
all of yesterday to be sure of you. If you come with me quietly,
I might be able to get you off with no punishment, if you agree
to go back to work on the hydrogen-plus bomb.'

'Science this guy talks at breakfast!' observed Mr. Melton,
half listening.

Simms went on, imperturbably. 'Think it over. You can't
escape. If you kill me, others will follow you.'

'We don't know what you're talking about.'

'Stop it!' cried Simms irritably. 'Use your intelligence! You know we can't let you get away with this escape. Other people in the year 2155 might get the same idea and do what you've done. We need people.'

'To fight your wars,' said William at last.

'Bill!'

'It's all right, Susan. We'll talk on his terms now. We can't escape.'

'Excellent,' said Simms. 'Really, you've both been incredibly romantic, running away from your responsibilities.'

'Running away from horror.'

'Nonsense. Only a war.'

'What are you guys talking about?' asked Mr. Melton.

Susan wanted to tell him. But you could only speak in generalities. The psychological bloc in your mind allowed that. Generalities, such as Simms and William were now discussing.

'Only *the* war,' said William. 'Half the world dead of leprosy bombs!'

'Nevertheless,' Simms pointed out, 'the inhabitants of the Future resent you two hiding on a tropical isle, as it were, while they drop off the cliff into hell. Death loves death, not life. Dying people love to know that others die with them. It is a comfort to learn you are not alone in the kiln, in the grave. I am the guardian of their collective resentment against you two.'

'Look at the guardian of resentments!' said Mr. Melton to his companions.

'The longer you keep me waiting, the harder it will go for you. We need you on the bomb project, Mr. Travis. Return now – no torture. Later, we'll force you to work, and after you've finished the bomb, we'll try a number of complicated new devices on you, sir.'

'I've a proposition,' said William. 'I'll come back with you if my wife stays here alive, safe, away from that war.'

Mr Simms considered it, 'All right. Meet me in the plaza in ten minutes. Pick me up in your car. Drive me to a deserted country spot. I'll have the Travel Machine pick us up there.'

'Bill!' Susan held his arm tightly.

'Don't argue.' He looked over at her. 'It's settled.' To Simms: 'One thing. Last night you could have gotten in our room and kidnapped us. Why didn't you?'

'Shall we say that I was enjoying myself?' replied Mr. Simms languidly, sucking his new cigar. 'I hate giving up this wonderful atmosphere, this sun, this vacation. I regret leaving behind the wine and the cigarettes. Oh, how I regret it. The plaza then, in ten minutes. Your wife will be protected and may stay here as long as she wishes. Say your good-byes.'

Mr. Simms arose and walked out.

'There goes Mr. Big Talk!' yelled Mr. Melton at the departing gentleman. He turned and looked at Susan. 'Hey. Someone's crying. Breakfast's no time for people to cry. Now *is* it?'

At nine-fifteen Susan stood on the balcony of their room, gazing down at the plaza. Mr. Simms was seated there, his neat legs crossed, on a delicate bronze bench. Biting the tip from a cigar, he lit it tenderly.

Susan heard the throb of a motor, and far up the street, out of a garage and down the cobbled hill, slowly, came William in his car.

The car picked up speed. Thirty, now forty, now fifty miles an hour. Chickens scattered before it.

Mr. Simms took off his white panama hat and mopped his pink forehead, put his hat back on, and then saw the car.

It was rushing sixty miles an hour, straight on for the plaza. 'William!' screamed Susan.

The car hit the low plaza curb, thundering; it jumped up, sped across the tiles toward the green bench where Mr. Simms now dropped his cigar, shrieked, flailed his hands, and was hit by the car. His body flew up and up in the air, and down and down, crazily, into the street.

On the far side of the plaza, one front wheel broken, the car stopped. People were running.

Susan went in and closed the balcony doors.

*

They came down the Official Palace steps together, arm in arm, their faces pale, at twelve noon.

'*Adiós señor*,' said the mayor behind them. '*Señora*.'

They stood in the plaza where the crowd was pointing at the blood.

'Will they want to see you again?' asked Susan.

'No, we went over and over it. It was an accident. I lost control of the car. I wept for them. God knows I had to get my relief out somewhere. I *felt* like weeping. I hated to kill him. I've never wanted to do anything like that in my life.'

'They won't prosecute you?'

'They talked about it, but no. I talked faster. They believe me. It was an accident. It's over.'

'Where will we go? Mexico City? Uruapan?'

'The car's in the repair shop. It'll be ready at four this afternoon. Then we'll get the hell out.'

'Will we be followed? Was Simms working alone?'

'I don't know. We'll have a little head start on them, I think.'

The film people were coming out of the hotel as they approached. Mr. Melton hurried up, scowling. 'Hey, I heard what happened. Too bad. Everything okay now? Want to get your mind off it? We're doing some preliminary shots up the street. You want to watch, you're welcome. Come on, do you good.'

They went.

They stood on the cobbled street while the film camera was being set up. Susan looked at the road leading down and away, and the highway going to Acapulco and the sea, past pyramids and ruins and little adobe towns with yellow walls, blue walls, purple walls and flaming bourgainvillea, and she thought, We shall take the roads, travel in clusters and crowds, in markets, in lobbies, bribe police to sleep near, keep double locks, but always the crowds, never alone again, always afraid the next person who passes may be another Simms. Never knowing if we've tricked and lost the Searchers. And always up ahead, in the Future, they'll wait for us to be brought back, waiting with their bombs to burn us and disease to rot us, and their police to tell us to roll over, turn around, jump through the hoop! And so we'll keep running through the forest, and we'll never ever stop or sleep well again in our lives.

A crowd gathered to watch the film being made. And Susan watched the crowd and the streets.

'Seen anyone suspicious?'

'No. What time is it?'

'Three o'clock. The car should be almost ready.'

The test film was finished at three forty-five. They all walked down to the hotel, talking. William paused at the garage. 'The car'll be ready at six,' he said, coming out, worried.

'But no later than that?'

'It'll be ready, don't worry.'

In the hotel lobby they looked around for other men travelling alone, men, who resembled Mr. Simms, men with new haircuts and too much cigarette smoke and cologne smell about them, but the lobby was empty. Going up the stairs, Mr. Melton said, 'Well, it's been a long hard day. Who'd like to put a header on it? You folks? Martini? Beer?'

'Maybe one.'

The whole crowd pushed into Mr. Melton's room and the drinking began.

'Watch the time,' said William.

Time, thought Susan. If only they had time. All she wanted was to sit in the plaza all of a long bright day in October, with not a worry or a thought, with the sun on her face and arms, her eyes closed, smiling at the warmth, and never move. Just sleep in the Mexican sun, and sleep warmly and easily and slowly and happily for many, many days. . . .

Mr. Melton opened the champagne.

'To a very beautiful lady, lovely enough for films,' he said, toasting Susan. 'I might even give you a test.'

She laughed.

'I mean it,' said Melton. 'You're very nice. I could make you a movie star.'

'And take me to Hollywood?' cried Susan.

'Get the hell out of Mexico, sure!'

Susan glanced at William and he lifted an eyebrow and

nodded. It would be a change of scene, clothing, locale, name, perhaps; and they would be travelling with eight other people, a good shield against any interference from the Future.

'It sounds wonderful,' said Susan.

She was feeling the champagne now. The afternoon was slipping by; the party was whirling about her. She felt safe and good and alive and truly happy for the first time in many years.

'What kind of film would my wife be good for?' asked William, refilling his glass.

Melton appraised Susan. The party stopped laughing and listened.

'Well, I'd like to do a story of suspense,' said Melton. 'A story of a man and wife, like yourselves.'

'Go on.'

'Sort of a war story, maybe,' said the director, examining the colour of his drink against the sunlight.

Susan and William waited.

'A story about a man and wife who live in a little house on a little street in the year 2155, maybe,' said Melton. 'This is *ad lib*, understand. But this man and wife are faced with a terrible war, super-plus hydrogen bombs, censorship, death in that year, and – here's the gimmick – they escape into the Past, followed by a man who they think is evil, but who is only trying to show them what their duty is.'

William dropped his glass to the floor.

Mr. Melton continued: 'And this couple take refuge with a group of film people whom they learn to trust. Safety in numbers, they say to themselves.'

Susan felt herself slip down into a chair. Everyone was watching the director. He took a little sip of wine. 'Ah, that's a fine wine. Well, this man and woman, it seems, don't realize how important they are to the Future. The man, especially, is the keystone to a new bomb metal. So the Searchers, let's call them, spare no trouble or expense to find, capture, and take home the man and wife, once they get them totally alone, in a hotel room, where no one can see. Strategy. The Searchers work alone, or in groups of eight. One trick or another will do it. Don't you think it would make a wonderful film, Susan? Don't you, Bill?' He finished his drink.

Susan sat with her eyes straight ahead of her.

'Have a drink?' said Mr. Melton.

William's gun was out and fired three times, and one of the men fell, and the others ran forward. Susan screamed. A hand was clamped to her mouth. Now the gun was on the floor and William was struggling, held.

Mr. Melton said, 'Please,' standing there where he had stood, blood showing on his fingers. 'Let's not make matters worse.'

Someone pounded on the hall door.

'Let me in!'

'The manager,' said Mr. Melton dryly. He jerked his head. 'Everyone, let's move!'

'Let me in! I'll call the police!'

Susan and William looked at each other quickly, and then at the door.

'The manager wishes to come in,' said Mr. Melton. 'Quick!'

A camera was carried forward. From it shot a blue light which encompassed the room instantly. It widened out and the people of the party vanished, one by one.

'Quickly!'

Outside the window, in the instant before she vanished, Susan saw the green land and the purple and yellow, and blue and crimson walls and the cobbles flowing down like a river, a man upon a burro riding into the warm hills, a boy drinking Orange Crush, she could feel the sweet liquid in her throat, a man standing under a cool plaza tree with a guitar, she could feel her hand upon the strings, and, far away, the sea, the blue and tender sea, she could feel it roll her over and take her in.

And then she was gone. Her husband was gone.

The door burst wide open. The manager and his staff rushed in.

The room was empty.

'But they were just here! I saw them come in, and now – gone!' cried the manager. 'The windows are covered with iron grating. They couldn't get out that way!'

In the late afternoon the priest was summoned and they

opened the room again and aired it out, and had him sprinkle holy water through each corner and give it his blessing.

'What shall we do with these?' asked the charwoman.

She pointed to the closet, where there were 67 bottles of chartreuse, cognac, *crême de cacao*, absinthe, vermouth, tequila, 106 cartons of Turkish cigarettes, and 198 yellow boxes of fifty-cent pure Havana-filled cigars. . . .

THE VISITOR

Saul Williams awoke to the still morning. He looked wearily out of his tent and thought about how far away Earth was. Millions of miles, he thought. But then what could you do about it? Your lungs were full of the 'blood rust'. You coughed all the time.

Saul arose this particular morning at seven o'clock. He was a tall man, lean, thinned by his illness. It was a quiet morning on Mars, with the dead sea bottom flat and silent – no wind on it. The sun was clear and cool in the empty sky. He washed his face and ate breakfast.

After that he wanted very much to be back on Earth. During the day he tried every way that it was possible to be in New York City. Sometimes, if he sat right and held his hands a certain way, he did it. He could almost smell New York. Most of the time, though, it was impossible.

Later in the morning Saul tried to die. He lay on the sand and told his heart to stop. It continued beating. He imagined himself leaping from a cliff or cutting his wrists, but laughed to himself – he knew he lacked the nerve for either act.

Maybe if I squeeze tight and think about it enough, I'll just sleep and never wake, he thought. He tried it. An hour later he awoke with a mouth full of blood. He got up and spat it out and felt very sorry for himself. This blood rust – it filled your mouth and your nose; it ran from your ears, your fingernails; and it took a year to kill you. The only cure was shoving you in a rocket and shooting you out to exile on Mars. There was no known cure on Earth, and remaining there would contaminate and kill others. So here he was, bleeding all the time, and lonely.

Saul's eyes narrowed. In the distance, by an ancient city ruin, he saw another man lying on a filthy blanket.

When Saul walked up, the man on the blanket stirred weakly.

'Hello, Saul,' he said.

'Another morning,' said Saul. 'Christ, I'm lonely!'

'It is an affliction of the rusted ones,' said the man on the blanket, not moving, very pale and as if he might vanish if you touched him.

'I wish to God,' said Saul, looking down at the man, 'that you could at least talk. Why is it that intellectuals never get the blood rust and come up here?'

'It is a conspiracy against you, Saul,' said the man, shutting his eyes, too weary to keep them open. Once I had the strength to be an intellectual. Now, it is a job to think.'

'If only we could talk,' said Saul Williams.

The other man merely shrugged indifferently.

'Come tomorrow. Perhaps I'll have enough strength to talk about Aristotle then. I'll try. Really I will.' The man sank down under the worn tree. He opened one eye. 'Remember, once we did talk on Aristotle, six months ago, on that good day I had.'

'I remember,' said Saul, not listening. He looked at the dead sea. 'I wish I were as sick as you, then maybe I wouldn't worry about being an intellectual. Then maybe I'd get some peace.'

'You'll get just as bad as I am now in about six months,' said the dying man. 'Then you won't care about anything but sleep and more sleep. Sleep will be like a woman to you. You'll always go back to her, because she's fresh and good and faithful and she always treats you kindly and the same. You only wake up so you can think about going back to sleep. It's a nice thought.' The man's voice was a bare whisper. Now it stopped and a light breathing took over.

Saul walked off.

Along the shores of the dead sea, like so many emptied bottles flung up by some long-gone wave, were the huddled bodies of sleeping men. Saul could see them all down the curve of the empty sea. One, two, three — of all of them sleeping alone, most of them worse off than he, each with his little cache of food, each grown into himself, because social converse was weakening and sleep was good.

At first there had been a few nights around mutual campfires. And they had all talked about Earth. That was the only thing they talked about. Earth and the way the waters ran in town creeks and what home-made strawberry pie tasted like and how New York looked in the early morning coming over on the Jersey ferry in the salt wind.

I want Earth, thought Saul. I want it so bad it hurts. I want something I can never have again. And they all want it, and it hurts them not to have it. More than food or a woman or anything, I just want Earth. This sickness puts women away for ever; they're not things to be wanted. But Earth, yes. That's a thing for the mind and not the weak body.

The bright metal flashed on the sky.

Saul looked up.

The bright metal flashed again.

A minute later the rocket landed on the sea bottom. A valve opened, a man stepped out, carrying his luggage with him. Two other men, in protective germicide suits accompanied him, bringing out vast cases of food, setting up a tent for him.

Another minute and the rocket returned to the sky. The exile stood alone.

Saul began to run. He hadn't run in weeks, and it was very tiring, but he ran and yelled.

'Hello, hello!'

The young man looked Saul up and down when he arrived.

'Hello. So this is Mars. My name's Leonard Mark.'

'I'm Saul Williams.'

They shook hands. Leonard Mark was very young – only eighteen; very blond, pink-faced, blue-eyed and fresh in spite of his illness.

'How are things in New York?' said Saul.

'Like this,' said Leonard Mark. And he looked at Saul.

New York grew up out of the desert, made of stone and filled with March winds. Neons exploded in electric colour. Yellow taxis glided in a still night. Bridges rose and tugs chanted in the midnight harbours. Curtains rose on spangled musicals.

Saul put his hands to his head, violently.

'Hold on, hold on!' he cried. 'What's happening to me? What's wrong with me? I'm going crazy!'

Leaves sprouted from trees in Central Park, green and new. On the pathway, Saul strolled along, smelling the air.

'Stop it, stop it, you fool!' Saul shouted at himself. He pressed his forehead with his hands. 'This can't be'!

'It is,' said Leonard Mark.

The New York towers faded. Mars returned. Saul stood on the empty sea bottom, staring limply at the young newcomer.

'You,' he said, putting his hand out to Leonard Mark. 'You did it. You did it with your mind.'

'Yes,' said Leonard Mark.

Silently they stood facing each other. Finally, trembling, Saul seized the other exile's hand and wrung it again and again, saying, 'Oh, but I'm glad you're here. You can't know how glad I am!'

They drank their rich brown coffee, from the tin cups.

It was high noon. They had been talking all through the warm morning time.

'And this ability of yours?' said Saul over his cup, looking steadily at the young Leonard Mark.

'It's just something I was born with,' said Mark, looking into his drink. 'My mother was in the blow-up of London back in '57. I was born ten months later. I don't know what you'd call my ability. Telepathy and thought transference, I suppose. I used to have an act. I travelled all around the world. Leonard Mark, the mental marvel, they said on the bill-boards, I I was pretty well off. Most people thought I was a charlatan. You know what people think of theatrical folks. Only I knew I was really genuine, but I didn't let anybody know. It was safer not to let it get around too much. Oh, a few of my close friends knew about my *real* ability. I had a lot of talents that will come in handy now that I'm here on Mars.'

'You sure scared the hell out of me,' said Saul, his cup rigid in his hand. 'When New York came right up out of the ground that way, I thought I was insane.'

'It's a form of hypnotism which affects all of the sensual

organs at once – eyes, ears, nose, mouth, skin – all of them.
What would you like to be doing now most of all?'

Saul put down his cup. He tried to hold his hands very
steady. He wet his lips. 'I'd like to be in a little creek I used to
swim in in Mellin Town, Illinois, when I was a kid. I'd like
to be stark-naked and swimming.'

'Well,' said Leonard Mark and moved his head ever so little.

Saul fell back on the sand, his eyes shut.

Leonard Mark sat watching him.

Saul lay on the sand. From time to time his hands moved,
twitched excitedly. His mouth spasmed open; sounds issued
from his tightening and relaxing throat.

Saul began to make slow movements of his arms, out and
back, out and back, gasping with his head to one side, his arms
going and coming slowly on the warm air, stirring the yellow
sand under him, his body turning slowly over.

Leonard Mark quietly finished his coffee. While he drank he
kept his eyes on the moving, whispering Saul lying there on the
dead sea bottom.

'All right,' said Leonard Mark.

Saul sat up, rubbing his face.

After a moment he told Leonard Mark, 'I *saw* the creek. I
ran along the bank and I took off my clothes,' he said breathlessly, his smile incredulous. 'And I *dived in* and swam
around!'

'I'm pleased,' said Leonard Mark.

'Here!' Saul reached into his pocket and drew forth his last
bar of chocolate. 'This is for *you*.'

'What's this?' Leonard Mark looked at the gift. 'Chocolate?
Nonsense, I'm not doing this for pay. I'm doing it because it
makes you happy. Put that thing back in your pocket before I
turn it into a rattlesnake and it bites you.'

'Thank you, thank you!' Saul put it away. 'You don't know
how good that water was.' He fetched the coffee-pot. 'More?'

Pouring the coffee, Saul shut his eyes a moment.

I've got Socrates here, he thought, Socrates and Plato, and
Nietzsche and Schopenhauer. This man, by his talk, is a genius.
By his talent, he's incredible! Think of the long, easy days

and the cool nights of talk we'll have. It won't be a bad year at all. Not half.

He spilled the coffee.

'What's wrong?'

'Nothing.' Saul himself was confused, startled.

We'll be in Greece, he thought. In Athens. We'll be in Rome, if we want, when we study the Roman writers. We'll stand in the Parthenon and the Acropolis. It won't be just talk, but it'll be a place to be, besides. This man can do it. He has the power to do it. When we talk the plays of Racine, he can make a stage and players and all of it for me. By Christ, this is better than life ever was! How much better to be sick and here than well on Earth without these abilities! How many people have ever seen a Greek drama played in a Greek amphitheatre in the year 31 B.C.?

And if I ask, quietly and earnestly, will this man take on the aspect of Schopenhauer and Darwin and Bergson and all the other thoughtful men of the ages . . .? Yes, why not? To sit and talk with Nietzsche in person, with Plato himself . . .!

There was only one thing wrong. Saul felt himself swaying.

The other men. The other sick ones along the bottom of this dead sea.

In the distance men were moving, walking towards them. They had seen the rocket flash, land, dislodge a passenger. Now they were coming, slowly, painfully, to greet the new arrival.

Saul was cold. 'Look,' he said. 'Mark, I think we'd better head for the mountains.

'Why?'

'See those men coming? Some of them are insane.'

'Really?'

'Yes.'

'Isolation and all make them that way?'

'Yes, that's it. We'd better get going.'

'They don't look very dangerous. They move slowly.'

'You'd be surprised.'

Mark looked at Saul. 'You're trembling. Why's that?'

'There's no time to talk,' said Saul, getting up swiftly. 'Come on. Don't you realize what'll happen once they discover your talent? They'll fight over you. They'll kill each other – kill you – for the right to own you.'

'Oh, but I don't belong to anybody,' said Leonard Mark. He looked at Saul. 'No. Not even you.'

Saul jerked his head. 'I didn't even think of that.'

'Didn't you now?' Mark laughed.

'We haven't time to argue,' answered Saul, eyes blinking, cheeks blazing. 'Come on!'

'I don't want to. I'm going to sit right here until those men show up. You're a little too possessive. My life's my own.'

Saul felt an ugliness in himself. His face began to twist. 'You *heard* what I said.'

'How very quickly you changed from a friend to an enemy,' observed Mark.

Saul hit at him. It was a neat quick blow, coming down.

Mark ducked aside, laughing. 'No, you don't!'

They were in the centre of Times Square. Cars roared, hooting, upon them. Buildings plunged up, hot, into the blue air.

'It's a lie!' cried Saul, staggering under the visual impact.

'For God's sake, don't, Mark! The men are coming. You'll be killed!'

Mark sat there on the pavement, laughing at his joke. 'Let them come. I can fool them all!'

New York distracted Saul. It was meant to distract – meant to keep his attention with its unholy beauty, after so many months away from it. Instead of attacking Mark he could only stand, drinking in the alien but familiar scene.

He shut his eyes. 'No.' And fell forward, dragging Mark with him. Horns screamed in his ears. Brakes hissed and caught violently. He smashed at Mark's chin.

Silence.

Mark lay on the sea bottom.

Taking the unconscious man in his arms, Saul began to run, heavily.

New York was gone. There was only the wide soundlessness of the dead sea. The men were closing in around him. He headed for the hills with his precious cargo, with New York and green country and fresh springs and old friends held in his arms. He fell once and struggled up. He did not stop running.

Night filled the cave. The wind wandered in and out, tugging at the small fire, scattering ashes.

Mark opened his eyes. He was tied with ropes and leaning against the dry wall of the cave, facing the fire.

Saul put another stick on the fire, glancing now and again with a cat-like nervousness at the cave entrance.

'You're a fool.'

Saul started.

'Yes,' said Mark, 'you're a fool. They'll find us. If they have to hunt for six months they'll find us. They saw New York, at a distance, like a mirage. And us in the centre of it. It's too much to think they won't be curious and follow our trail.'

'I'll move on with you then,' said Saul, staring into the fire.

'And they'll come after.'

'Shut up!'

Mark smiled. 'Is that the way to speak to your wife?'

'You heard me!'

'Oh, a fine marriage this is – your greed and my mental ability. What do you want to see now? Shall I show you a few more of your childhood scenes?'

Saul felt the sweat coming out on his brow. He didn't know if the man was joking or not. 'Yes,' he said.

'All right,' said Mark, 'watch!'

Flame gushed out of the rocks. Sulphur choked him. Pits of brimstone exploded, concussions rocked the cave. Heaving up, Saul coughed and blundered, burned, withered by hell!

Hell went away. The cave returned.

Mark was laughing.

Saul stood over him. 'You,' he said coldly, bending down.

'What else do you expect?' cried Mark. 'To be tied up, toted off, made the intellectual bride of a man insane with loneliness – do you think I enjoy this?'

'I'll untie you if you promise not to run away.'

'I couldn't promise that. I'm a free agent. I don't belong to anybody.'

Saul got down on his knees. 'But you've *got* to belong, do you hear? You've *got* to belong. I can't let you go away!'

'My dear fellow, the more you say things like that, the more remote I am. If you'd had any sense and done things intelligently, we'd have been friends. I'd have been glad to do you these little hypnotic favours. After all, they're no trouble for me to conjure up. Fun, really. But you've botched it. You wanted me all to yourself. You were afraid the others would take me away from you. Oh, how mistaken you were. I have enough power to keep them all happy. You could have shared me, like a community kitchen. I'd have felt quite like a god among children, being kind, doing favours, in return for which you might bring me little gifts, special tidbits of food.'

'I'm sorry, I'm sorry!' Saul cried. 'But I know those men too well.'

'Are you any different? Hardly! Go out and see if they're coming. I thought I heard a noise.'

Saul ran. In the cave entrance he cupped his hands, peering down into the night-filled gully. Dim shapes stirred. Was it only the wind blowing the roving clumps of weeds? He began to tremble – a fine, aching tremble.

'I don't see anything.' He came back into an empty cave.

He stared at the fireplace. 'Mark!'

Mark was gone.

There was nothing but the cave, filled with boulders, stones, pebbles, the lonely fire flickering, the wind sighing. And Saul standing there, incredulous and numb.

'Mark! Mark! Come back!'

The man had worked free of his bonds, slowly, carefully, and using the ruse of imagining he heard other men approaching, had gone – where?

The cave was deep, but ended in a blank wall. And Mark could not have slipped past him into the night. How then?

Saul stepped around the fire. He drew his knife and approached a large boulder that stood against the cave wall. Smiling, he pressed the knife against the boulder. Smiling, he tapped the knife there. Then he drew his knife back to plunge it into the boulder.

'Stop!' shouted Mark.

The boulder vanished. Mark was there.

Saul suspended his knife. The fire played on his cheeks. His eyes were quite insane.

'It didn't work,' he whispered. He reached down and put his hands on Mark's throat and closed his fingers. Mark said nothing, but moved uneasily in the grip, his eyes ironic, telling things to Saul that Saul knew.

If you kill me, the eyes said, where will all your dreams be? If you kill me, where will all the streams and brook trout be? Kill me, kill Plato, kill Aristotle, kill Einstein; yes, kill all of us! Go ahead, strangle me. I dare you.

Saul's fingers released the throat.

Shadows moved into the cave mouth.

Both men turned their heads.

The other men were there. Five of them, haggard with travel, panting, waiting in the outer rim of light.

'Good evening,' called Mark, laughing. 'Come in, come in, gentlemen!'

By dawn the arguments and ferocities still continued. Mark sat among the glaring men, rubbing his wrists newly released from his bonds. He created a mahogany-panelled conference hall and a marble table at which they all sat, ridiculously bearded, evil smelling, sweating and greedy men, eyes bent upon their treasure.

'The way to settle it,' said Mark at last, 'is for each of you to have certain hours of certain days for appointments with me. I'll treat you all equally. I'll be city property, free to come and go. That's fair enough. As for Saul here, he's on probation. When he's proved he can be a civil person once more, I'll give him a treatment or two. Until that time, I'll have nothing more to do with him.'

The other exiles grinned at Saul.

'I'm sorry,' Saul said. 'I didn't know what I was doing. I'm all right now.'

'We'll see,' said Mark. 'Let's give ourselves a month, shall we?'

The other men grinned at Saul.

Saul said nothing. He sat staring at the floor of the cave.

'Let's see now,' said Mark. 'On Mondays it's your day, Smith.'

Smith nodded.

'On Tuesdays I'll take Peter there, for an hour or so.'

Peter nodded.

'On Wednesdays I'll finish up with Johnson, Holtzman, and Jim, here.'

The last three men looked at each other.

'The rest of the week I'm to be left strictly alone, do you hear?' Mark told them. 'A little should be better than nothing. If you don't obey, I won't perform at all.'

'Maybe we'll *make* you perform,' said Johnson. He caught the other men's eye. 'Look, we're five against his one. We can make him do anything we want. If we co-operate, we've got a great thing here.'

'Don't be idiots,' Mark warned the other men.

'Let me talk,' said Johnson. 'He's telling *us* what he'll do. Why don't we tell *him*! Are we bigger than him, or not? And him threatening not to perform! Well, just let me get a sliver of wood under his toenails and maybe burn his fingers a bit with a steel file, and we'll see if he performs! Why shouldn't we have performances, I want to know, every night in the week?'

'Don't listen to him!' said Mark. 'He's crazy. He can't be depended on. You know what he'll do, don't you? He'll get you all off guard, one by one, and kill you; yes, kill all of you, so that when he's done, he'll be alone – just him and me! That's his sort.'

The listening men blinked. First at Mark, then at Johnson.

'For that matter,' observed Mark, 'none of you can trust the others. This is a fool's conference. The minute your back is turned one of the other men will murder you. I dare say, at the week's end, you'll all be dead or dying.'

A cold wind blew into the mahogany room. It began to dissolve and became a cave once more. Mark was tired of his joke. The marble table splashed and rained and evaporated.

The men gazed suspiciously at each other with little bright

animal eyes. What was spoken was true. They saw each other in the days to come, surprising one another, killing – until that last lucky one remained to enjoy the intellectual treasure that walked among them.

Saul watched them and felt alone and disquieted. Once you have made a mistake, how hard to admit your wrongness, to go back, start fresh. They were *all* wrong. They had been lost a long time. Now they were worse than lost.

'And to make matters very bad,' said Mark at last, 'one of you has a gun. All the rest of you have only knives. But one of you, I know, has a gun.'

Everybody jumped up. 'Search!' said Mark. 'Find the one with the gun or you're all dead!'

That did it. The men plunged wildly about, not knowing whom to search first. Their hands grappled, they cried out, and Mark watched them in contempt.

Johnson fell back, feeling in his jacket. 'All right,' he said. 'We might as well have it over now! Here, you, Smith.'

And he shot Smith through the chest. Smith fell. The other men yelled. They broke apart. Johnson aimed and fired twice more.

'Stop!' cried Mark.

New York soared up around them, out of rock and cave and sky. Sun glinted on high towers. The elevated thundered; tugs blew in the harbour. The green lady stared across the bay, a torch in her hand.

'Look, you fools!' said Mark. Central Park broke out constellations of spring blossoms. The wind blew fresh-cut lawn smells over them in a wave.

And in the centre of New York, bewildered, the men stumbled. Johnson fired his gun three times more. Saul ran forward. He crashed against Johnson, bore him down, wrenched the gun away. It fired again.

The men stopped milling.

They stood. Saul lay across Johnson. They ceased struggling.

There was a terrible silence. The men stood watching. New

York sank down into the sea. With a hissing, bubbling, sighing; with a cry of ruined metal and old time, the great structures leaned, warped, flowed, collapsed.

Mark stood among the buildings. Then, like a building, a neat red hole drilled into his chest, wordless, he fell.

Saul lay staring at the men, at the body.

He got up, the gun in his hand.

Johnson did not move – was afraid to move.

They all shut their eyes and opened them again, thinking that by so doing they might reanimate the man who lay before them.

The cave was cold.

Saul stood up and looked, remotely, at the gun in his hand. He took it and threw it far out over the valley and did not watch it fall.

They looked down at the body as if they could not believe it. Saul bent down and took hold of the limp hand. 'Leonard!' he said softly. 'Leonard!' He shook the hand. 'Leonard!'

Leonard Mark did not move. His eyes were shut; his chest had ceased going up and down. He was getting cold.

Saul got up. 'We've killed him,' he said, not looking at the men. His mouth was filling with a raw liquor now. 'The only one we didn't want to kill, we killed.' He put his shaking hand to his eyes. The other men stood waiting.

'Get a spade,' said Saul. 'Bury him.' He turned away. 'I'll have nothing to do with you.'

Somebody walked off to find a spade.

Saul was so weak he couldn't move. His legs were grown into the earth, with roots feeding deep of loneliness and fear and the cold of the night. The fire had almost died out and now there was only the double moonlight riding over the blue mountains.

There was the sound of someone digging in the earth with a spade.

'We don't need him anyhow,' said somebody, much too loudly.

The sound of digging went on. Saul walked off slowly and let himself slide down the side of a dark tree until he reached and was sitting blankly on the sand, his hands blindly in his lap.

Sleep, he thought. We'll all go to sleep now. We have that much, anyway. Go to sleep and try to dream of New York and all the rest.

He closed his eyes wearily, the blood gathering in his nose and his mouth and in his quivering eyes.

'How did he do it?' he asked in a tired voice. His head fell forward on his chest. 'How did he bring New York up here and make us walk around in it? Let's try. It shouldn't be too hard. Think! Think of New York,' he whispered, falling down into sleep. 'New York and Central Park and then Illinois in the spring, apple blossom and green grass.'

It didn't work. It wasn't the same. New York was gone and nothing he could do would bring it back. He would rise every morning and walk on the dead sea looking for it, and walk for ever around Mars, looking for it, and never find it. And finally lie, too tired to walk trying to find New York in his head, but not finding it.

The last thing he heard before he slept was the spade rising and falling and digging a hole into which, with a tremendous crash of metal and golden mist and odour and colour and sound, New York collapsed, fell, and was buried.

He cried all night in his sleep.

MARIONETTES, INC.

They walked slowly down the street at about ten in the evening, talking calmly. They were both about thirty-five, both eminently sober.

'But why so early?' said Smith.

'Because,' said Braling.

'Your first night out in years and you go home at ten o'clock.'

'Nerves, I suppose.'

'What I wonder is how you ever managed it. I've been trying to get you out for ten years for a quiet drink. And now, on the one night, you insist on turning in early.'

'Mustn't crowd my luck,' said Braling.

'What did you do, put sleeping powder in your wife's coffee?'

'No, that would be unethical. You'll see soon enough.'

They turned a corner. 'Honestly, Braling, I hate to say this, but you *have* been patient with her. You may not admit it to me, but marriage has been awful for you, hasn't it?'

'I wouldn't say that.'

'It's got around, anyway, here and there, how she got you to marry her. That time back in 1979 when you were going to Rio—'

'Dear Rio. I never *did* see it after all my plans.'

'And how she tore her clothes and rumpled her hair and threatened to call the police unless you married her.'

'She always was nervous, Smith, understand.'

'It was more than unfair. You didn't love her. You told her as much, didn't you?'

'I recall that I was quite firm on the subject.'

'But you married her anyhow.'

'I had my business to think of, as well as my mother and father. A thing like that would have killed them.'

'And it's been ten years.'

'Yes,' said Braling, his grey eyes steady. 'But I think perhaps it might change now. I think what I've waited for has come about. Look here.'

He drew forth a long blue ticket.

"Why, it's a ticket for Rio on the Thursday rocket!'

'Yes, I'm finally going to make it.'

'But how wonderful! You *do* deserve it! But won't *she* object? Cause trouble?'

Braling smiled nervously. 'She won't know I'm gone. I'll be back in a month and no one the wiser, except you.'

Smith sighed. 'I wish I were going with you.'

'Poor Smith, *your* marriage hasn't exactly been roses, has it?'

'Not exactly, married to a woman who overdoes it. I mean, after all, when you've been married ten years, you don't expect a woman to sit on your lap for two hours every evening, call you at work twelve times a day and talk baby talk. And it seems to me that in the last month she's gotten worse. I wonder if perhaps she isn't just a little simple-minded?'

'Ah, Smith, always the conservative. Well, here's my house. Now, would you like to know my secret? How I made it out this evening?'

'Will you really tell?'

'Look up there!' said Braling.

They both stared up through the dark air.

In the window above them, on the second floor, a shade was raised. A man about thirty-five years old, with a touch of grey at either temple, sad grey eyes, and a small thin moustache looked down at them.

'Why, that's *you*!' cried Smith.

'Sh-h-h, not so loud!' Braling waved upward. The man in the window gestured significantly and vanished.

'I must be insane,' said Smith.

'Hold on a moment.'

They waited.

The street door of the apartment opened and the tall spare gentleman with the moustache and the grieved eyes came out to meet them.

'Hello, Braling,' he said.

'Hello, Braling,' said Braling.

They were identical.

Smith stared. 'Is this your twin brother? I never knew—'

'No, no,' said Braling quietly. 'Bend close. Put your ear to Braling Two's chest.'

Smith hesitated and then leaned forward to place his head against the uncomplaining ribs.

Tick-tick-tick-tick-tick-tick-tick-tick.

'Oh, no! It *can't* be!'

'It is.'

'Let me listen again.'

Tick-tick-tick-tick-tick-tick-tick-tick.

Smith staggered back and fluttered his eyelids, appalled. He reached out and touched the warm hands and the cheeks of the thing.

'Where'd you get him?'

'Isn't he excellently fashioned?'

'Incredible. Where?'

'Give the man your card, Braling Two.'

Braling Two did a magic trick and produced a white card:

MARIONETTES, INC.

Duplicate self or friends; new humanoid plastic 1990 models, guaranteed against all physical wear. From $7,600 to our $15,000 de luxe model.

'No,' said Smith.

'Yes,' said Braling.

'Naturally,' said Braling Two.

'How long has this gone on?'

'I've had him for a month. I keep him in the cellar in a toolbox. My wife never goes downstairs, and I have the only lock and key to that box. Tonight I said I wished to take a walk to buy a cigar. I went down to the cellar and took Braling Two out of his box and sent him back up to sit with my wife while I came on out to see you, Smith.'

'Wonderful! He even *smells* like you: Bond Street and Mel-achrinos!'

It may be splitting hairs, but I think it highly ethical. After all, what my wife wants most of all is *me*. This marionette *is* me to the hairiest detail. I've been home all evening. I shall be home with her for the next month. In the meantime another gentleman will be in Rio after ten years of waiting. When I return from Rio, Braling Two here will go back in his box.'

Smith thought that over a minute or two. 'Will he walk around without sustenance for a month?' he finally asked.

'For six months if necessary. And he's built to do everything – eat, sleep, perspire – everything, natural as natural is. You'll take good care of my wife, won't you, Braling Two?'

'Your wife is rather nice,' said Braling Two. 'I've grown rather fond of her.'

Smith was beginning to tremble. 'How long has Mari-onettes, Inc., been in business?'

'Secretly, for two years.'

'Could I – I mean, is there a possibility—' Smith took his friend's elbow earnestly. 'Can you tell me where I can get one, a robot, a marionette, for myself? You *will* give me the address, won't you?'

'Here you are.'

Smith took the card and turned it round and round. 'Thank you,' he said. 'You don't know what this means. Just a little respite. A night or so, once a month even. My wife loves me so much she can't bear to have me gone an hour. I love her dearly, you know, but remember the old poem: "Love will fly if held too lightly, love will die if held too tightly." I just want her to relax her grip a little bit.'

'You're lucky, at least, that your wife loves you. Hate's my problem. Not so easy.'

'Oh, Nettie loves me madly. It will be my task to make her love me comfortably.'

'Good luck to you, Smith. Do drop around while I'm in Rio. It will seem strange, if you suddenly stop calling by, to my wife. You're to treat Braling Two here, just like me.'

'Right! Good-bye. And thank you.'

Smith went smiling down the street. Braling and Braling Two turned and walked into the apartment hall.

On the crosstown bus Smith whistled softly, turning the white card in his fingers:

Clients must be pledged to secrecy, for while an act is pending in Congress to legalize Marionettes, Inc., it is still a felony, if caught, to use one.

'Well,' said Smith.

Clients must have a mould made of their body and a colour index check of their eyes, lips, hair, skin, etc. Clients must expect to wait for two months until their model is finished.

Not so long, thought Smith. Two months from now my ribs will have a chance to mend from the crushing they've taken. Two months from now my hand will heal from being so constantly held. Two months from now my bruised underlip will begin to reshape itself. I don't mean to sound *ungrateful* ... He flipped the card over.

Marionettes, Inc., is two years old and has a fine record of satisfied customers behind it. Our motto is 'No Strings Attached'. Address: 43 South Wesley Drive.

The bus pulled to his stop; he alighted, and while humming up the stairs he thought, Nettie and I have fifteen thousand in our joint bank account. I'll just slip eight thousand out as a business venture, you might say. The marionette will probably pay back my money, with interest, in many ways. Nettie needn't know. He unlocked the door and in a minute was in the bedroom. There lay Nettie, pale, huge, and piously asleep.

'Dear Nettie.' He was almost overwhelmed with remorse at her innocent face there in the semi-darkness. 'If you were awake you would smother me with kisses and coo in my ear. Really, you make me feel like a criminal. You have been such a good, loving wife. Sometimes it is impossible for me to believe you married me instead of that Bud Chapman you once liked. It seems that in the last month you have loved me more wildly than *ever* before.'

Tears came to his eyes. Suddenly, he wished to kiss her, confess his love, tear up the card, forget the whole business. But as he moved to do this, his hand ached and his ribs cracked and groaned. He stopped, with a pained look in his eyes, and turned away. He moved out into the hall and through the dark rooms. Humming, he opened the kidney desk in the library and filched the bankbook. 'Just take eight thousand dollars is all,' he said. 'No more than that.' He stopped. 'Wait a minute.'

He rechecked the bankbook frantically. 'Hold on here!' he cried. 'Ten thousand dollars is missing!' He leaped up. 'There's only five thousand left! What's she done? What's Nettie done with it? More hats, more clothes, more perfume! Oh, wait – I know! She bought that little house on the Hudson she's been talking about for months, without so much as a by your leave!'

He stormed into the bedroom, righteous and indignant. What did she mean, taking their money like this? He bent over her. 'Nettie!' he shouted. 'Nettie, wake up!'

She did not stir. 'What've you done with my money!' he bellowed.

She stirred fitfully. The light from the street flushed over her beautiful cheeks.

There was something about her. His heart throbbed violently. His tongue dried. He shivered. His knees suddenly turned to water. He collapsed. 'Nettie, Nettie!' he cried. 'What've you done with my money!'

And then, the horrid thought. And then the terror and the loneliness engulfed him. And then the fever and dis-illusionment. For, without desiring to do so, he bent forward and yet forward again until his fevered ear was resting firmly and irrevocably upon her round pink bosom. 'Nettie!' he cried.

Tick-tick-tick-tick-tick-tick-tick-tick-tick-tick-tick.

As Smith walked away down the avenue in the night, Bral-

ing and Braling Two turned in at the door to the apartment.
'I'm glad he'll be happy too,' said Braling.

'Yes,' said Braling Two abstractedly.

'Well, it's the cellar box for you, 'B-Two.' Braling guided the
other creature's elbow down the stairs to the cellar.

'That's what I want to talk to you about,' said Braling Two,
as they reached the concrete floor and walked across it. 'The
cellar. I don't like it. I don't like that toolbox.'

'I'll try and fix up something more comfortable.'

'Marionettes are made to move, not lie still. How would you
like to lie in a box most of the time?'

'Well—'

'You wouldn't like it all. I keep running. There's no way to
shut me off. I'm perfectly alive and I have feelings.'

'It'll only be a few days now. I'll be off to Rio and you won't
have to stay in the box. You can live upstairs.'

Braling Two gestured irritably. 'And when you come back
from having a good time, back in the box I go.'

Braling said, 'They didn't tell me at the marionette shop that
I'd get a difficult specimen.'

'There's a lot they don't know about us,' said Braling Two.
'We're pretty new. And we're sensitive. I hate the idea of you
going off and laughing and lying in the sun in Rio while we're
stuck here in the cold.'

'But I've wanted that trip all my life,' said Braling quietly.

'He squinted his eyes and could see the sea and the mountains and the yellow sand. The sound of the waves was good to
his inward mind. The sun was fine on his bared shoulders. The
wine was most excellent.

'*I'll* never get to go to Rio,' said the other man. 'Have you
thought of that?'

'No, I—'

'And another thing. Your wife.'

'What about her?' asked Braling, beginning to edge toward
the door.

'I've grown quite fond of her.'

'I'm glad you're enjoying your employment.' Braling licked
his lips nervously.

'I'm afraid you don't understand. I think – I'm in love with her.'

Braling took another step and froze. 'You're *what*?'

'And I've been thinking,' said Braling Two, 'how nice it is in Rio and how I'll never get there, and I've thought about your wife and – I think we could be very happy.'

'Th-that's nice.' Braling strolled as casually as he could to the cellar door. 'You won't mind waiting a moment, will you? I have to make a phone call.'

'To whom?' Braling Two frowned.

'No one important.'

'To Marionettes, Incorporated? To tell them to come get me?'

'No, no – nothing like that!' He tried to rush out the door. A metal-firm grip seized his wrists. 'Don't run!'

'Take your hands off!'

'No.'

'Did my wife put you up to this?'

'No.'

'Did she guess? Did she talk to you? Does she know? Is *that* it?' He screamed. A hand clapped over his mouth.

'You'll never know, will you?' Braling Two smiled delicately. 'You'll never know.'

Braling struggled. 'She *must* have guessed; she *must* have affected you!'

Braling Two said, 'I'm going to put you in the box, lock it, and lose the key. Then I'll buy another Rio ticket for your wife.'

'Now, now, wait a minute. Hold on. Don't be rash. Let's talk this over!'

'Good-bye, Braling.'

Braling stiffened. 'What do you mean, "good-bye"?'

Ten minutes later Mrs. Braling awoke. She put her hand to her cheek. Someone had just kissed it. She shivered and looked up. 'Why – you haven't done that in years,' she murmured.

'We'll see what we can do about that,' someone said.

THE CITY

The city waited twenty thousand years.

The planet moved through space and the flowers of the fields grew up and fell away, and still the city waited; and the rivers of the planet rose and waned and turned to dust.

Still the city waited. The winds that had been young and wild grew old and serene, and the clouds of the sky that had been ripped and torn were left alone to drift in idle whitenesses. Still the city waited.

The city waited with its windows and its black obsidian walls and its sky towers and its unpennanted turrets, with its untrod streets and its untouched doorknobs, with not a scrap of paper or a fingerprint upon it. The city waited while the planet arced in space, following its orbit about a blue-white sun, and the seasons passed from ice to fire and back to ice and then to green fields and yellow summer meadows.

It was on a summer afternoon in the middle of the twenty thousandth year that the city ceased waiting.

In the sky a rocket appeared.

The rocket soared over, turned, came back, and landed in the shale meadow fifty yards from the obsidian wall.

There were booted footsteps in the thin grass and calling voices from men within the rocket to men without.

'Ready?'

'All right, men. Careful! Into the city. Jensen, you and Hutchinson patrol ahead. Keep a sharp eye.'

The city opened secret nostrils in its black walls and a steady suction vent deep in the body of the city drew storms of air back through channels, through thistle filters and dust collectors, to a fine and tremblingly delicate series of coils and webs which glowed with silver light. Again and again the immense suctions occurred; again and again the odours from the meadow were borne upon warm winds into the city.

'Fire odour, the scent of a fallen meteor, hot metal. A ship has come from another world. The brass smell, the dusty fire smell of burned powder, sulphur, and rocket brimstone.'

This information, stamped on tapes which sprocketed into slots, slid down through yellow cogs into further machines.

Click-chakk-chakk-chakk.

A calculator made the sound of a metronome. Five, six, seven, eight, nine. Nine men! An instantaneous typewriter inked this message on tape which slithered and vanished.

Clickety-click-chakk-chakk.

The city awaited the soft tread of their rubberoid boots.

The great city nostrils dilated again.

The smell of butter. In the city air, from the stalking men, faintly, the aura which wafted to the great Nose broke down into memories of milk, cheese, ice cream, butter, the effluvium of a dairy economy.

Click-click.

'Careful, men!'

'Jones, get your gun out. Don't be a fool!'

'The city's dead; why worry?'

'You can't tell.'

Now, at the barking talk, the Ears awoke. After centuries of listening to winds that blew small and faint, of hearing leaves strip from trees and grass grow softly in the time of melting snows, now the Ears oiled themselves in a self-lubrication, drew taut, great drums upon which the heartbeat of the invaders might pummel and thud delicately as the tremor of a gnat's wing. The Ears listened and the Nose siphoned up great chambers of odour.

The perspiration of frightened men arose. There were islands of sweat under their arms, and sweat in their hands as they held their guns.

The Nose sifted and worried this air, like a connoisseur busy with an ancient vintage.

Chikk-chikk-chakk-click.

Information rotated down on parallel check tapes. Perspiration; chlorides such and such per cent; sulphates so-and-so; urea nitrogen, ammonia nitrogen, *thus*: creatinine, sugar, lactic acid, *there*!

Bells rang. Small totals jumped up.

The Nose whispered, expelling the tested air. The great Ears listened:

'I think we should go back to the rocket, Captain.'

'I give the orders, Mr. Smith!'

'Yes, sir.'

'You, up there! Patrol! *See* anything?'

'Nothing, sir. Looks like it's been dead a long time!'

'You see, Smith? Nothing to fear.'

'I don't like it. I don't know why. You ever feel you've seen a place before? Well, this city's too familiar.'

'Nonsense. This planetary system's billions of miles from Earth; we couldn't possibly've been here ever before. Ours is the only light-year rocket in existence.'

'That's how I feel, anyway sir. I think we should get out.'

The footsteps faltered. There was only the sound of the intruders' breath on the still air.

The Ear heard and quickened. Rotors glided, liquids glittered in small creeks through the valves and blowers. A formula and a concoction – one followed another. Moments later, responding to the summons of the Ear and Nose, through giant holes in the city walls a fresh vapour blew out over the invaders.

'Smell *that*, Smith? Ahh. Green grass. Ever smell anything better? By God, I just like to stand here and smell it.'

Invisible chlorophyll blew among the standing men.

'*Ahh!*'

The footsteps continued.

'Nothing wrong with *that* eh, Smith? Come on!'

The Ear and Nose relaxed a billionth of a fraction. The counter-move had succeeded. The pawns were proceeding forward.

Now the cloudy Eyes of the city moved out of fog and mist.

'Captain, the windows!'

'What?'

'Those house windows, there! I saw them move!'

'*I* didn't see it'

'They shifted. They changed colour. From dark to light.'

'Look like ordinary square windows to me.'

Blurred objects focused. In the mechanical ravines of the city
oiled shafts plunged, balance wheels dipped over into green oil
pools. The window frames flexed. The windows gleamed.

Below, in the street, walked two men, a patrol, followed, at a
safe interval, by seven more. Their uniforms were white, their
faces as pink as if they had been slapped; their eyes were blue.
They walked upright, upon hind legs, carrying metal weapons.
Their feet were booted. They were males, with eyes, ears,
mouths, noses.

The windows trembled. The windows thinned. They dilated
imperceptibly, like the irises of numberless eyes.

'I tell you, Captain, it's the windows!'

'Get along.'

'I'm going back, sir.'

'What?'

'I'm going back to the rocket.'

'Mr. Smith!'

'I'm not falling into any trap!'

'Afraid of an empty city?'

The others laughed, uneasily.

'Go on, laugh!'

The street was stone-cobbled, each stone three inches wide,
six inches long. With a move unrecognizable as such, the street
settled. It weighed the invaders.

In a machine cellar a red wand touched a numeral: 178
pounds ... 210, 154, 201, 198 – each man weighed, registered
and the record spooled down into a correlative darkness.

Now the city was fully awake!

Now the vents sucked and blew air, the tobacco odour from
the invaders' mouths, the green soap scent from their hands.
Even their eyeballs had a delicate odour. The city detected it,
and this information formed totals which scurried down to total
other totals. The crystal windows glittered, the Ear tautened
and skinned the drum of its hearing tight, tighter – all the

senses of the city swarming like a fall of unseen snow, counting the respiration and the dim hidden heartbeats of the men, listening, watching, tasting.

For the streets were like tongues, and where the men passed, the taste of their heels ebbed down through stone pores to be calculated on litmus. This chemical totality, so subtly collected, was appended to the now increasing sums waiting the final calculation among the whirling wheels and whispering spokes.

Footsteps. Running.

'Come back! Smith!'

'No, blast you!'

'Get him, men!'

Footsteps rushing.

A final test. The city, having listened, watched, tasted, felt, weighed, and balanced, must peform a final task.

A trap flung wide in the street. The captain, unseen to the others, running, vanished.

Hung by his feet, a razor drawn across his throat, another down his chest, his carcass instantly emptied of its entrails, exposed upon a table under the street, in a hidden cell, the captain died. Great crystal microscopes stared at the red twines of muscle; bodiless fingers probed the still pulsing heart. The flaps of his sliced skin were pinned to the table while hands shifted parts of his body like a quick and curious player of chess, using the red pawns and the red pieces.

Above on the street the men ran. Smith ran, men shouted. Smith shouted, and below in this curious room blood flowed into capsules, was shaken, spun, shoved on smear slides under further microscopes, counts made, temperatures taken, heart cut in seventeen sections, liver and kidneys expertly halved. Brain was drilled and scooped from bone socket, nerves pulled forth like the dead wires of a switchboard, muscles plucked for elasticity, while in the electric subterrene of the city the Mind at last totalled out its grandest total and all of the machinery ground to a monstrous and momentary halt.

The total.

These are men. These are men from a far world, a certain

planet, and they have certain eyes, certain ears, and they walk upon legs in a specified way and carry weapons and think and fight, and they have particular hearts and all such organs as are recorded from long ago.

Above, men ran down the street toward the rocket.

Smith ran.

The total.

These are our enemies. These are the ones we have waited for twenty thousand years to see again. These are the men upon whom we waited to visit revenge. Everything totals. These are the men of a planet called Earth, who declared war upon Taollan twenty thousand years ago, who kept us in slavery and ruined us and destroyed us with a great disease. Then they went off to live in another galaxy to escape that disease which they visited upon us after ransacking our world. They have forgotten that war and that time, and they have forgotten us. But we have not forgotten them. These are our enemies. This is certain. Our waiting is done.

'Smith, come back!'

Quickly. Upon the red table, with the spread-eagled captain's body empty, new hands began a fight of motion. Into the wet interior were placed organs of copper, brass, silver, aluminium, rubber and silk; spiders spun gold web which was stung into the skin; a heart was attached, and into the skull case was fitted a platinum brain which hummed and fluttered small sparkles of blue fire, and the wires led down through the body to the arms and legs. In a moment the body was sewn tight, the incisions waxed, healed at neck and throat and about the skull — perfect, fresh, new.

The captain sat up and flexed his arms.

'Stop!'

On the street the captain reappeared, raised his gun and fired.

Smith fell, a bullet in his heart.

The other men turned.

The captain ran to them.

'That fool! Afraid of a city!'

They looked at the body of Smith at their feet.

They looked at their captain, and their eyes widened and narrowed.

'Listen to me,' said the captain. 'I have something important to tell you.'

Now the city, which had weighed and tasted and smelled them, which had used all its powers save one, prepared to use its final ability, the power of speech. It did not speak with the rage and hostility of its massed walls or towers, nor with the bulk of its cobbled avenues and fortresses of machinery. It spoke with the quiet voice of one man.

'I am no longer your captain,' he said. 'Nor am I a man.'

The men moved back.

'I am the city,' he said, and smiled.

'I've waited two hundred centuries,' he said. 'I've waited for the sons of the sons of the sons to return.'

'Captain, sir!'

'Let me continue. Who built me? The city. The men who died built me. The old race who once lived here. The people whom the Earthmen left to die of a terrible disease, a form of leprosy with no cure. And the men of that old race, dreaming of the day when Earthmen might return, built this city, and the name of this city was and is Revenge, upon the planet of Darkness, near the shore of the Sea of Centuries, by the Mountains of the Dead; all very poetic. This city was to be a balancing machine, a litmus, an antenna to test all future space travellers. In twenty thousand years only two other rockets landed here. One from a distant galaxy called Ennt, and the inhabitants of that craft were tested, weighed, found wanting, and let free, unscathed, from the city. As were the visitors in the second ship. But today! At long last, you've come! The revenge will be carried out to the last detail. Those men have been dead two hundred centuries, but they left a city here to welcome you.'

'Captain, sir, you're not feeling well. Perhaps you'd better come back to the ship, sir.'

The city trembled.

The pavements opened and the men fell, screaming. Falling, they saw bright razors flash to meet them!

Time passed. Soon came the call:

'Smith?'

'Here!'

'Jensen?'

'Here!'

'Jones, Hutchinson, Springer?'

'Here, here, here!'

They stood by the door of the rocket.

'We return to Earth immediately.'

'Yes, sir!'

The incisions on their necks were invisible, as were their hidden brass hearts and silver organs and the fine golden wire of their nerves. There was a faint electric hum from their heads.

'At the double!'

Nine men hurried the golden bombs of disease culture into the rocket.

'These are to be dropped on Earth.'

'Right, sir!'

The rocket valve slammed. The rocket jumped into the sky.

As the thunder faded, the city lay upon the summer meadow. Its glass eyes were dulled over. The Ear relaxed, the great nostril vents stopped, the streets no longer weighed or balanced, and the hidden machinery paused in its bath of oil.

In the sky the rocket dwindled.

Slowly, pleasurably, the city enjoyed the luxury of dying.

ZERO HOUR

Oh, it was to be so jolly! What a game! Such excitement they hadn't known in years. The children catapulted this way and that across the green lawns, shouting at each other, holding hands, flying in circles, climbing trees, laughing. Overhead the rockets flew, and beetle cars whispered by on the streets, but the children played on. Such fun, such tremulous joy, such tumbling and hearty screaming.

Mink ran into the house, all dirty and sweat. For her seven years she was loud and strong and definite. Her mother, Mrs. Morris, hardly saw her as she yanked out drawers and rattled pans and tools into a large sack.

'Heavens, Mink, what's going on?'

'The most exciting game ever!' gasped Mink, pink-faced.

'Stop and get your breath,' said the mother.

'No, I'm all right,' gasped Mink. 'Okay I take these things, Mom?'

'But don't dent them,' said Mrs. Morris.

'Thank you, thank you!' cried Mink, and boom! she was gone, like a rocket.

Mrs. Morris surveyed the fleeing tot. 'What's the name of the game?'

'Invasion!' said Mink. The door slammed.

In every yard on the street children brought out knives and forks and pokers and old stovepipes and can-openers.

It was an interesting fact that this fury and bustle occurred only among the younger children. The older ones, those ten years and more, disdained the affair and marched scornfully off on hikes or played a more dignified version of hide-and-seek on their own.

Meanwhile, parents came and went in chromium beetles. Repairmen came to repair the vacuum elevators in houses, to fix fluttering television sets or hammer upon stubborn food-delivery tubes. The adult civilization passed and repassed the busy youngsters, jealous of the fierce energy of the wild tots, tolerantly amused at their flourishings, longing to join in themselves.

'This and this and *this*,' said Mink, instructing the others with their assorted spoons and wrenches. 'Do that, and bring *that* over here. No! *Here*, ninny! Right. Now, get back while I fix this.' Tongue in teeth, face wrinkled in thought. Like that. See?'

'Yayyy!' shouted the kids.

Twelve-year-old Joseph Connors ran up.

'Go away,' said Mink straight at him.

'I wanna play,' said Joseph.

'Can't!' said Mink.

'Why not?'

'You'd just make fun of us.'

'Honest, I wouldn't.'

'No. We know *you*. Go away or we'll kick you.'

Another twelve-year-old boy whirred by on little motor skates. 'Hey, Joe! Come on! Let them sissies play!'

Joseph showed reluctance and a certain wistfulness. 'I *want* to play,' he said.

'You're old,' said Mink firmly.

'Not *that* old,' said Joe sensibly.

'You'd only laugh and spoil the Invasion.'

The boy on the motor skates made a rude lip noise. 'Come on, Joe! Them and their fairies! Nuts!'

Joseph walked off slowly. He kept looking back, all down the block.

Mink was already busy again. She made a kind of apparatus with her gathered equipment. She had appointed another little girl with a pad and pencil to take down notes in painful slow scribbles. Their voices rose and fell in the warm sunlight.

All around them the city hummed. The streets were lined with good green and peaceful trees. Only the wind made a conflict across the city, across the country, across the continent. In a thousand other cities there were trees and children and avenues, businessmen in their quiet offices taping their voices, or watching television. Rockets hovered like darning needles in the blue sky. There was the universal, quiet conceit and easiness of men accustomed to peace, quite certain there would never be trouble again. Arm in arm, men all over earth were a united front. The perfect weapons were held in equal trust by all nations. A situation of incredibly beautiful balance had been brought about. There were no traitors among men, no unhappy ones, no disgruntled ones; therefore the world was based upon a stable ground. Sunlight illumined half the world and the trees drowsed in a tide of warm air.

Mink's mother, from her upstairs window, gazed down.

The children. She looked upon them and shook her head. Well, they'd eat well, sleep well, and be in school on Monday. Bless their vigorous little bodies. She listened.

Mink talked earnestly to someone near the rose bush – though there was no one there.

These odd children. And the little girl, what was her name? Anna? Anna took notes on a pad. First, Mink asked the rosebush a question, then called the answer to Anna.

'Triangle,' said Mink.

'What's a tri,' said Anna with difficulty, 'angle?'

'Never mind,' said Mink.

'How you spell it?' asked Anna.

'T-r-i—' spelled Mink slowly, then snapped, 'Oh, spell it yourself!' She went on to other words. 'Beam,' she said.

'I haven't got tri,' said Anna, 'angle down yet!'

'Well, hurry, hurry!' cried Mink.

Mink's mother leaned out of the upstairs window. 'A-n-g-l-e,' she spelled down at Anna.

'Oh, thanks, Mrs. Morris,' said Anna.

'Certainly,' said Mink's mother and withdrew, laughing, to dust the hall with an electro-duster magnet.

The voices wavered on the shimmery air. 'Beam,' said Anna. Fading.

'Four-nine-seven-A-and-B-and-X,' said Mink, far away, seriously. 'And a fork and a string and a – hex-hex-agony – hexagonal!'

At lunch Mink gulped milk at one toss and was at the door. Her mother slapped the table.

'You sit right back down,' commanded Mrs. Morris. 'Hot soup in a minute.' She poked a red button on the kitchen butler, and ten seconds later something landed with a bump in the rubber receiver. Mrs. Morris opened it, took out a can with a pair of aluminium holders, unsealed it with a flick, and poured hot soup into a bowl.

During all this Mink fidgeted. 'Hurry, Mom! This is a matter of life and death! Aw—'

'I was the same way at your age. Always life and death. I know.'

Mink banged away at the soup.

'Slow down,' said Mom.

'Can't,' said Mink. 'Drill's waiting for me.'

'Who's Drill? What a peculiar name,' said Mom.

'You don't know him,' said Mink.

'A new boy in the neighbourhood?' asked Mom.

'He's new all right,' said Mink. She started on her second bowl.

'Which one is Drill?' asked Mom.

'He's around,' said Mink evasively. 'You'll make fun. Everybody pokes fun. Gee, darn.'

'Is Drill shy?'

'Yes. No. In a way. Gosh, Mom, I got to run if we want to have the Invasion!'

'Who's invading what?'

'Martians invading Earth Well, not exactly Martians. They're – I don't know. From up.' She pointed with her spoon.

'And *inside*,' said Mom, touching Mink's feverish brow.

Mink rebelled. 'You're laughing! You'll kill Drill and everybody.'

'I didn't mean to,' said Mom. 'Drill's a Martian?'

'No. He's – well – maybe from Jupiter or Saturn or Venus. Anyway, he's had a hard time.'

'I imagine.' Mrs. Morris hid her mouth behind her hand.

'They couldn't figure a way to attack Earth.'

'We're impregnable,' said Mom in mock seriousness.

'That's the word Drill used! Impreg— That was the word, Mom.'

'My, my, Drill's a brilliant little boy. Two-bit words.'

'They couldn't figure a way to attack, Mom. Drill says – he says in order to make a good fight you got to have a new way of surprising people. That way you win. And he says also you got to have help from your enemy.'

'A fifth column,' said Mom.

'Yeah. That's what Drill said. And they couldn't figure a way to surprise Earth or get help.'

'No wonder. We're pretty darn strong.' Mom laughed, cleaning up. Mink sat there, staring at the table, seeing what she was talking about.

'Until, one day,' whispered Mink melodramatically, 'they thought of children!'

'*Well!*' said Mrs. Morris brightly.

'And they thought of how grown-ups are so busy they never look under rose bushes or on lawns!'

'Only for snails and fungus.'

'And then there's something about dim-dims.'

'Dim-dims?'

'Dimens-shuns.'

'Dimensions?'

'Four of 'em! And there's something about kids under nine and imagination. It's real funny to hear Drill talk.'

Mrs. Morris was tired. 'Well, it must be funny. You're keeping Drill waiting now. It's getting late in the day and, if you want to have your Invasion before your supper bath, you'd better jump.'

'Do I have to take a bath?' growled Mink.

'You do! Why is it children hate water? No matter what age you live in children hate water behind the ears!'

'Drill says I won't have to take baths,' said Mink.

'Oh, he does, does he?'

'He told all the kids that. No more baths. And we can stay up till ten o'clock and go to two televisor shows on Saturday 'stead of one!'

'Well, Mr. Drill better mind his p's and q's. I'll call up his mother and—'

Mink went to the door. 'We're having trouble with guys like Pete Britz and Dale Jerrick. They're growing up. They make fun. They're worse than parents. They just won't believe in Drill. They're so snooty, 'cause they're growing up. You'd think they'd know better. They were little only a coupla years ago. I hate them worst. We'll kill them *first*.'

'Your father and I last?'

'Drill says you're dangerous. Know why? 'Cause you don't believe in Martians! They're going to let *us* run the world. Well, not just us, but the kids over in the next block, too. I might be queen.' She opened the door.

'Mom?'

'Yes?'

'What's lodge-ick?'

'Logic? Why, dear, logic is knowing what things are true and not true.'

'He *mentioned* that,' said Mink. 'And what's im-pres-sion-able?' It took her a minute to say it.

'Why, it means—' Her mother looked at the floor, laughing gently. 'It means – to be a child, dear.'

'Thanks for lunch!' Mink ran out, then stuck her head back in. 'Mom, I'll be sure you won't be hurt much, really!'

'Well, thanks,' said Mom.

Slam went the door.

At four o'clock the audio-visor buzzed. Mrs. Morris flipped the tab. 'Hello, Helen!' she said in welcome.

'Hello, Mary. How are things in New York?'

'Fine. How are things in Scranton? You look tired.'

'So do you. The children. Underfoot,' said Helen.

Mrs. Morris sighed. 'My Mink too. The super-Invasion'

Helen laughed. 'Are your kids playing that game too?'

'Lord, yes. Tomorrow it'll be geometrical jacks and motorized hopscotch. Were we this bad when we were kids in '48?'

'Worse. Japs and Nazis. Don't know how my parents put up with me. Tomboy.'

'Parents learn to shut their ears.'

A silence.

'What's wrong, Mary?' asked Helen.

Mrs. Morris's eyes were half closed; her tongue slid slowly thoughtfully, over her lower lip. 'Eh?' She jerked. 'Oh, nothing. Just thought about *that*. Shutting ears and such. Never mind. Where were we?'

'My boy Tim's got a crush on some guy named – *Drill*, I think it was.'

'Must be a new password. Mink likes him too.'

'Didn't know it had got as far as New York. Word of mouth, I imagine. Looks like a scrap drive. I talked to Josephine and she said her kids – that's in Boston – are wild on this new game. It's sweeping the country.'

At this moment Mink trotted into the kitchen to gulp a glass of water. Mrs. Morris turned. 'How're things going?'

'Almost finished,' said Mink.

'Swell,' said Mrs. Morris. 'What's *that*?'

'A yo-yo,' said Mink. 'Watch.'

She flung the yo-yo down its string. Reaching the end it—

It vanished.

'See?' said Mink. 'Ope!' Dibbling her finger, she made the yo-yo reappear and zip up the string.

'Do that again,' said her mother.

'Can't. Zero hour's five o'clock! 'Bye.' Mink exited, zipping her yo-yo.

On the audio-visor, Helen laughed. 'Tim brought one of those yo-yos in this morning, but when I got curious he said he wouldn't show it to me, and when I tried to work it, finally, it wouldn't work.'

'You're not *impressionable*,' said Mrs. Morris.

'What?'

'Never mind. Something I thought of. Can I help you, Helen?'

'I wanted to get that black-and-white cake recipe—'

The hour drowsed by. The way waned. The sun lowered in

the peaceful blue sky. Shadows lengthened on the green lawns.
The laughter and excitement continued. One little girl ran
away, crying. Mrs. Morris came out the front door.

'Mink was that Peggy Ann crying?'

Mink was bent over in the yard, near the rosebush. 'Yeah.
She's a scarebaby. We won't let her play, now. She's getting too
old to play. I guess she grew up all of a sudden.'

'Is that why she cried? Nonsense. Give me a civil answer,
young lady, or inside you come!'

Mink whirled in consternation, mixed with irritation. 'I can't
quit now. It's almost time. I'll be good. I'm sorry.'

'Did you hit Peggy Ann?'

'No, honest. You ask her. It was something – well, she's just
a scaredy pants.'

The ring of children drew in around Mink where she scowled
at her work with spoons and a kind of square-shaped ar-
rangement of hammers and pipes. 'There and there,' murmured
Mink.

'What's wrong?' said Mrs. Morris.

'Drill's stuck. Half-way. If we could only get him all the way
through it'd be easier. Then the others could come through
after him.'

'Can I help?'

'No'm, thanks. I'll fix it.'

'All right. I'll call you for your bath in half an hour. I'm tired
of watching you.'

She went in and sat in the electric relaxing chair, sipping a
little beer from a half-empty glass. The chair massaged her
back. Children, children. Children and love and hate, side by
side. Sometimes children loved you, hated you – all in half a
second. Strange children, did they ever forget or forgive the
whippings and the harsh, strict words of command? She wondered. How can you ever forget or forgive those over and above
you, those tall and silly dictators?

Time passed. A curious, waiting silence came upon the
street, deepening.

Five o'clock. A clock sang softly somewhere in the house in a quiet musical voice: 'Five o'clock – five o'clock. Time's a-wasting. Five o'clock-' and purred away into silence.

Zero hour.

Mrs. Morris chuckled in her throat. Zero hour.

A beetle car hummed into the driveway. Mr. Morris. Mrs. Morris smiled. Mr. Morris got out of the beetle, locked it, and called hello to Mink at her work. Mink ignored him. He laughed and stood for a moment watching the children. Then he walked up the front steps.

'Hello, darling.'

'Hello, Henry.'

She strained forward on the edge of the chair, listening. The children were silent. Too silent.

He emptied his pipe, refilled it. 'Swell day. Makes you glad to be alive.'

Buzz.

'What's that?' asked Henry.

'I don't know.' She got up suddenly, her eyes widening. She was going to say something. She stopped it. Ridiculous. Her nerves jumped. 'Those children haven't anything dangerous out there, have they?' she said:

'Nothing but pipes and hammers. Why?'

'Nothing electrical?'

'Heck, no,' said Henry. 'I looked.'

She walked to the kitchen. The buzzing continued. 'Just the same, you'd better go tell them to quit. It's after five. Tell them—' Her eyes widened and narrowed. 'Tell them to put off their Invasion until tomorrow.' She laughed, nervously.

The buzzing grew louder.

'What are they up to? I'd better go look, all right.'

The explosion!

The house shook with dull sound. There were other explosions in other yards on other streets.

Involuntarily, Mrs. Morris screamed. 'Up this way!' she cried senselessly, knowing no sense, no reason. Perhaps she saw something from the corners of her eyes; perhaps she smelled a new odour or heard a new noise. There was no time to argue with Henry to convince him. Let him think her insane. Yes, insane! Shrieking, she ran upstairs. He ran after her to see what she was up to. 'In the attic!' she screamed. 'That's where it is!' It was only a poor excuse to get him in the attic in time. Oh, God – in time!

Another explosion outside. The children screamed with delight, as if at a great fireworks display.

'It's not in the attic!' cried Henry. 'It's outside!'

'No, no!' Wheezing, gasping, she fumbled at the attic door. 'I'll show you. Hurry! I'll show you!'

They tumbled into the attic. She slammed the door, locked it, took the key, threw it into a far, cluttered corner.

She was babbling wild stuff now. It came out of her. All the subconscious suspicion and fear that had gathered secretly all afternoon and fermented like a wine in her. All the little revelations and knowledges and sense that had bothered her all day and which she had logically and carefully and sensibly rejected and censored. Now it exploded in her and shook her to bits.

'There, there,' she said, sobbing against the door. 'We're safe until tonight. Maybe we can sneak out. Maybe we can escape!'

Henry blew up too, but for another reason. 'Are you crazy? Why'd you throw that key away? Damn it, honey!'

'Yes, yes, I'm crazy, if it helps, but stay here with me!'

'I don't know how in hell I *can* get out!'

'Quiet. They'll hear us. Oh, God, they'll find us soon enough—'

Below them, Mink's voice. The husband stopped. There was a great universal humming and sizzling, a screaming and giggling. Downstairs the audio-television buzzed and buzzed insistently, alarmingly, violently. *Is that Helen calling?* thought Mrs. Morris. *And is she calling about what I think she's calling about?*

Footsteps came into the house. Heavy footsteps.

'Who's coming in my house?' demanded Henry angrily. 'Who's tramping around down there?'

Heavy feet. Twenty, thirty, forty, fifty of them. Fifty persons crowding into the house. The humming. The giggling of the children. 'This way!' cried Mink, below.

'Who's downstairs?' roared Henry. 'Who's there!'

'Hush. Oh, nonononononono!' said his wife weakly, holding him. 'Please, be quiet. They might go away.'

'Mom?' called Mink. 'Dad?' A pause. 'Where are you?'

Heavy footsteps, heavy, heavy, very *heavy* footsteps, came up the stairs. Mink leading them.

'Mom?' A hesitation. 'Dad?' A waiting, a silence.

Humming. Footsteps toward the attic. Mink's first.

They trembled together in silence in the attic, Mr. and Mrs. Morris. For some reason the electric humming, the strange odour and the alien sound of eagerness in Mink's voice finally got through to Henry Morris too. He stood, shivering, in the dark silence, his wife beside him.

'Mom! Dad!'

Footsteps. A little humming sound. The attic-lock melted. The door opened. Mink peered inside, tall blue shadows behind her.

'Peekaboo,' said Mink.

THE PLAYGROUND

He had often walked by the playground on the way from his train and paid it no particular attention. He neither liked nor disliked it, he had no opinion of it. But his wife had looked at him across the breakfast table this morning and said, 'I'm going to start Jim at the playground this week. You know, the one down the street. Jim's old enough now.'

At his office, Mr. Charles Underhill had made a memorandum: *Look at playground.* And on the way home down the street from the train at four in the afternoon, he purposely folded his newspaper so he would not read himself past the playground.

Now, at four-ten in the late day, he moved slowly along the sidewalk and stopped at the playground gate.

At first there was nothing. And then, as his ears adjusted outward from his usual interior monologues, it was like turning the volume dial of a radio louder. And the scene before him, like a grey, blurred television image, came to a slow focus. Primarily, there were faint voices, faint cries, streaks and shadows, vague impressions. And then, as if someone had jolted the machine, there were screams, sharp visions, children dashing, children fighting, pummelling, bleeding, screaming! He saw the tiniest scabs on their faces and knees in amazing clarity.

Mr. Underhill stood there in the full volume of blasting sound, blinking. And then his nostrils took up where his eyes and ears left off.

He smelled the cutting odours of iodine, raw adhesive, and pink mercurochrome, so strong it was bitter to his tongue. The wind of iodine moving through the steely wire fence which glinted dully in the grey light of the overcast day. And the rushing children there, it was like hell cut loose in a great pintable machine, a colliding and banging and totalling of hits and pushes and rushes to a grand and as yet unforeseen total of brutalities. And was he mistaken or was the light of a strange intensity within the playground; everything seeming to possess four shadows, one dark one, and three subsidiaries, which made it impossible, strategically, to tell which way the small bodies were screaming until they bashed their targets. Yes, the oblique, pressing light made the entire playground seem deep, far away, and somehow remote from his touching it. Or perhaps it was the hard steel wire fence, not unlike certain park zoo barriers, beyond which anything might happen.

'A pen of misery, that's what it is,' said Mr. Underhill. 'Why do children insist on making life miserable for each other? It's nothing but torture to be a child.' He heard himself give a great relieved sigh. Thank God, childhood was over and done for him. No more pinchings, bruisings, shattered dreams and senseless excitements.

A gust of wind tore the paper from his hand and blew it through the gate. He went after it, down into the playground, three steps. Clutching it, he immediately retreated, heart pounding, for in the moment he had remained stranded in the playground's atmosphere he had felt his hat too large, his coat too cumbersome, his belt too loose, his shoes too big, he had felt like a small boy playing business man in his father's clothes, and the gate behind him had loomed impossibly large, while the sky itself pressed greyer at his eyes, and the scent of the iodine, like that of a feral tiger's mouth exhaled upon him, touched and blew his hair. He almost stumbled and fell, getting out of there!

He stood outside, like someone who has just emerged, shocked, from a terrible, cold sea.

'Hello, Charlie!'

He heard the voice and turned to see who had called him. There was the caller, on top a slide, a boy about nine years old, waving. 'Hello, Charlie!'

Mr. Charles Underhill raised a hand. 'But I don't *know* that boy,' he murmured. 'And why should he call me by my first name?'

The boy was smiling up in the murky air, and now, jostled by other yelling children, rushed shrieking down the slide.

Mr. Underhill stood bemused by what he saw. Now the playground was an immense iron industry whose sole product was pain, sorrow and sadism. If you stood here half an hour there wasn't a face in the entire enclosure that didn't wince, cry, redden with anger, or pale with fear, one minute or another. Really! Who said childhood was the best time of life, when in reality it was the most horrifying, the most merciless era, the barbaric time when there were no police to protect you, only parents preoccupied with themselves and the taller world. No, if he had his way, he gripped the fence with one fist, they'd nail a new sign here: TORQUEMADA'S GREEN.

And as for that boy, the one who had shouted at him, who was he? There was something familiar there, perhaps in the hidden bones, an echo of some old friend, probably the son of a successfully ulcered father.

And this is the playground where my son will play, thought Mr. Underhill, and shuddered.

Hanging his hat in the hall, checking his lean image in the watery mirror, Mr. Underhill felt wintry and tired. When his wife appeared, and his son came tapping on mousefeet, he greeted them with something less than full attention. The boy clambered thinly over him, playing KING OF THE HILL. And the father, fixing his gaze to the end of the cigar he was slowly lighting, finally cleared his throat and said, 'I've been thinking about that playground, Susan.'

'I'm taking Jim over tomorrow,' said his wife.

'Not really? That playground?'

His mind rebelled. The smell and look of the place were still vivid to him. That writhing world with its atmosphere of cuts and beaten noses, the air as full of pain as a dentist's office, and those horrid tic-tac-toes and hopscotches under his feet as he picked up his newspaper, horrid for no reason he could see!

'What's wrong with that playground?' asked his wife.

'Have you seen it?' He paused in confusion. 'Damn it, I mean, the children there. It's a Black Hole, that's what it is.'

'The children are clean and from well-to-do families.'

'Why, they shove and push like vulgar little Gestapos,' cried

Mr. Underhill. 'It'd be like shoving the child in a granary to be ground down into meal by a couple of two-ton grinders! Every time I think of Jim settling into that barbaric pit, I turn cold!'

'You know it's the only convenient centre.'

'They'll kill Jim. I saw some with all kinds of bats and clubs and guns. Good God, Jim'll be in splinters by the end of the first day. They'll have him on a spit with an orange in his mouth.'

'How you exaggerate!' She was laughing at him.

'I'm serious!'

'You can't live Jim's life for him, you know that. He has to learn the hard way. He's got to be beat up and beat others up; children are like that.'

'I don't *like* children like that.'

'It's the happiest time of life.'

'Nonsense! I used to look back on childhood with nostalgia. Now I realize I was a sentimental fool. It was nothing but scratching and beating and kicking and coming home a bleeding scab from head to foot. If I could possibly save Jim from that, I would.'

'That's impractical and anyway, thank God, impossible.'

'I won't have him near that place, I tell you. I'll have him grow up a neurotic recluse first.'

'Charlie!'

'I will! Those little beasts, you should've *seen* them! He's my only son, Jim is.' He felt the boy's skinny legs about his shoulders, the boy's delicate hands rumpling his hair. 'I won't have him butchered.'

'He'll get it in school, later. Better to let him get a little shoving about now, when he's three, so he's prepared for it.'

'I've thought of that, too.' Mr. Underhill fiercely held to his son's ankles that dangled like warm, thin sausages on either lapel. 'I might even get a private tutor for him!'

'Oh, Charles!'

They did not speak during dinner.

After dinner, he took Jim for a walk while his wife was washing the dishes. They strolled down past the playground under the dim street lamps. It was a cooling September night, with the first sniff of autumn in it. Next week, and the children would be raked in off the fields like so many leaves and set to burning in the schools, using their fire and energy for more constructive purposes. But they would be here after school, ramming about, making projectiles of themselves, exploding and crashing, leaving a wake of misery behind their miniature wars.

'Wanna go in,' said Jim, leaning against the cold wire fence, watching the horrible children beat each other and run.

'No, Jim, you don't want that.'

'Play,' said Jim, his eyes glassy with fascination, as he saw a large boy kick a small boy and the small boy kick a smaller boy to even things up.

'Play, Daddy.'

'Come along, Jim, you'll never get in that mess if *I* can help it.' Mr. Underhill tugged the small arm firmly.

'Play.' Jim was beginning to blubber now. His eyes were melting out of his cheeks. His face became a wrinkled orange of colour and feeling.

Some of the children heard the crying and glanced over. Underhill had the terrible sense of watching a den of foxes suddenly startled and looked up from the white hairy ruin of a dead rabbit. The mean yellow eyes, the conical chins, the white teeth, the dreadful wiry hair, the brambly sweaters, the iron-coloured hands covered with a day's battle dust.

They saw Jim and he was new. They didn't say anything, but as Jim cried louder and Mr. Underhill, by main force, dragged him like a cement bag along the walk, they watched the little boy. Mr. Underhill felt like pushing his fist at them and crying, 'You little beasts, you won't get *my* son!'

And then, with beautiful irrelevance, the boy at the top of the slide, the boy with the familiar face, called to him, waving.

'Hello, Charlie.'

Mr. Underhill paused and Jim stopped crying.

'See you later, Charlie.'

And the face of the boy way up there on that high slide, was suddenly like the face of Thomas Marshall, an old business friend who lived just around the block but whom he hadn't seen in years.

'See you later, Charlie.'

Later, later? What did the fool boy mean?

'I know *you*, Charlie!' called the boy. 'Hi!'

'What?' gasped Mr. Underhill.

'Tomorrow night, Charlie, hey!' And the boy fell off the slide and lay choking for breath, face like a cheese from the fall, while children jumped on him and tumbled over.

Mr. Underhill stood undecided for five seconds or more, until Jim thought to cry again and then, with the fox eyes upon them, in the first chill of autumn, he dragged Jim all the way home.

The next afternoon Mr. Underhill finished at the office early and took the three o'clock train, arriving out in Green Town at three-twenty-five, in plenty of time to drink in the brisk rays of the autumnal sun. Strange how one day it is suddenly autumn, he thought. One day it is summer and the next, how could you measure or tell it? Something about the temperature or smell? Or the sediment of age knocked loose from your bones during the night and circulating in your blood and heart, giving you a slight tremble and a chill? A year older, a year dying, was *that* it?

He walked up toward the playground, planning the future. It seemed you did more planning in autumn than any other season. This had to do with dying, perhaps. You thought of death and you automatically planned. Well, then, there was to be a tutor for Jim *that* was positive; none of those horrible schools for him. It would pinch the bank account a bit, but Jim would at least grow up a happy boy. They would pick and choose his friends. Any slambang bullies would be thrown out as soon as they so much as touched Jim. And as for this playground. Completely out of the question!

'Oh, hello, Charles.'

He looked up suddenly. Before him, at the entrance to the wire enclosure, stood his wife. He noted instantly that she called him Charles, instead of Dear. Last night's unpleasantness had not quite evaporated. 'Susan, what're you doing down here?'

She flushed guiltily and glanced in through the fence.

'You didn't!' he cried.

His eyes sought among the scrabbling, running, screaming children. 'Do you mean to say . . .?'

His wife nodded, half amused. 'I thought I'd bring him early—'

'Before I got home, so I wouldn't know is *that* it?'

That was it.

'Good God, Susan, where *is* he?'

'I just came to see.'

'You mean you left him there all afternoon?'

'Just half an hour while I shopped.'

'And you *left* him, good God!' Mr. Underhill flung his hand to his drained cheek. 'Well, come on, find him, get him out of there!'

They peered in together past the wire to where some boys charged about, to girls slapping each other, to a squabbling heap of children who seemed to take turns at getting off, taking a good run, and jumping one against another.

'That's where he is, I *know* it!' said Mr. Underhill.

Just then, across the field at full speed, sobbing and wailing, came Jim, with six boys after him. He fell, got up, ran, fell again, stumbled up, shrieking, and the boys behind him shot beans through metal shooters.

'I'll stuff those blowers up their noses!' cried Mr. Underhill. 'Come on, Jim! Run!'

Jim made it to the gate. Mr. Underhill caught him and it was like catching a rumpled, bloody wad of material. Jim's nose was bleeding and his pants were ripped and he was covered with grime.

'*There's* your playground,' said Mr. Underhill, bent to his knees, staring up from his son, patting him, to his wife, viciously. 'There's your sweet happy little innocents, your well-to-do piddling Fascists! Let me catch this boy in there again and there'll be hell. Come on, Jim. All right, you little bastards, get back there!' he shouted.

'We didn't do nothing,' said the children.

'What's the world coming to?' Mr. Underhill questioned the universe.

'Hi, Charlie,' said the strange boy, standing to one side. He waved casually and smiled

'Who's that?' asked Susan

'How in hell do *I* know?' snapped Mr. Underhill.

'Be seeing you, Charlie, so long,' called the boy.

Mr. Underhill marched his wife and child home.

'Take your hand off my elbow!' she said.

He was trembling, absolutely, continually trembling with rage when he got to bed. He had tried some coffee, but nothing stopped it. He wanted to beat their pulpy little brains out, those gross Cruikshank children; yes, that phrase fitted them, those fox-fiend, melancholy Cruikshank children, with all the guile and poison and slyness in their cold faces. In the name of all that was decent, what manner of child was this new generation? A bunch of cutters and hangers and kickers, a drove of bleeding, moronic thumb-screwers, with the sewage of neglect running in their veins? He lay violently jerking his head from one side of his hot pillow to the other, and at last got up and lit a cigarette, but it wasn't enough. He and Susan had had a huge battle when they got home. He had yelled at her and she had yelled back, peacock and peahen shrieking in a wilderness where law and order were insanities laughed at and forgotten.

He was ashamed. You didn't fight violence with violence, not if you were a gentleman. You talked calmly. But she didn't give him a chance, damn it! She wanted the boy put in a vice and squashed. She wanted him reamed and punctured and given the laying-on-of-hands. To be beaten from playground to kindergarten, to grammar school, to junior high, to high school. If he was lucky, in high school, the beatings and sadisms would refine themselves, the sea of blood and spittle would drain back down the shore of years and Jim would be left upon the edge of maturity, with God knows what outlook to the future, with a desire, perhaps, to be a wolf among wolves, a dog among dogs, a fiend among fiends. But there was enough of that in the world, already. And the very thought of the next ten or fifteen years of torture was enough to make Mr. Underhill cringe, he felt his own flesh impaled with a BB shot, stung, burned, fisted, scrounged, twisted, violated, and bruised. He quivered, like a jelly-fish hurled violently into a concrete-mixer. Jim would never survive it. Jim was too delicate for this horror.

'I've made up my mind,' said Susan, in bed. 'You needn't walk the room all night. Jim's not having a private tutor. He's going to school. And he's going back to that playground tomorrow and keep going back until he's learned to stand on his own two feet.'

'Let me alone.' Mr. Underhill dressed. Downstairs, he opened the front door. It was about five minutes to midnight as he walked swiftly down the street, trying to outdistance his rage and outrage. He knew Susan was right, of course. This was the world, you lived in it, you accepted it, but *that* was the very trouble! He had been through the mill already, he knew what it was to be a boy among lions, his own childhood had come rushing back to him the last few hours, a time of terror and violence, and now he could not bear to think of Jim going through it all, those long years, especially if you were a delicate child, through no fault of your own, your bones thin, your face pale, what could you expect but to be harried and chased?

He stopped by the playground which was still lit by one great overhead lamp. It was locked for the night, but that one light remained on until twelve. He wanted to tear the contemptible place down, rip up the steel fences, obliterate the slides, and say to the children, 'Go home! Play in your back yards!'

How ingenious, the cold, deep playground. You never knew where anyone lived. The boy who knocked your teeth out, who was *he*? Nobody knew. Where did he live? Nobody knew. How to find him? Nobody knew. Why, you could come here one day, beat the living tar out of some smaller child, and run on the next day to some *other* playground. They would never find you. From playground to playground, you could take your criminal tricks, with everyone forgetting you, since they never knew you. You could return to this playground a month later, and if the little child whose teeth you knocked out was there and recognized you, you could deny it. No, I'm not the one. Must be some other kid. This is my first time here! No, not me! And when his back is turned, knock him down. And run off down the nameless streets, a nameless person.

'What am I going to do?' asked Mr. Underhill. 'I can't buck Susan forever on this. Should we move to the country? I can't do that. But I can't have Jim here, either.'

'Hello, Charlie,' said a voice.

Mr. Underhill turned. Inside the fence, seated in the dirt, making diagrams with one finger in the cold dust, was the nine-year-old boy. He didn't look up. He said hello, Charlie, just sitting there, easily, in that world beyond the hard steel fence.

Mr. Underhill said, 'How do you know my name?'

'You're having a lot of trouble.' The boy crossed his legs comfortably, smiling.

'How'd you get in there so late? Who are you?'

'My name's Marshall—'

'Of course, Tom Marshall's son. Tommy. I *thought* you looked familiar.'

'More familiar than you think.' The boy laughed.

'How's your father, Tommy?'

'Have you seen him lately?' the boy asked.

'Briefly, on the street, a month ago.'

'How did he look?'

'What?'

'How did Mr. Marshall look?' asked the boy. It was strange he wouldn't say 'my Father'.

'He looked all right. Why?'

'I guess he's happy,' said the boy. Mr. Underhill saw the boy's arms and legs and they were covered with scabs and scratches.

'Aren't you going home, Tommy?'

'I sneaked out to see you. I just knew you'd come. You're afraid.'

Mr. Underhill didn't know what to say.

'Those little monsters,' he said at last.

'Maybe I can help you.' The boy made a dust triangle.

It was ridiculous. 'How?'

'You'd give anything, wouldn't you, if you could spare Jim all this? You'd trade places with him if you could?'

Mr. Underhill nodded, frozen.

'Well, you come down here tomorrow afternoon at four. Then I can help you.'

'How do you mean, help?'

'I can't tell you outright,' said the boy. 'It has to do with the playground. Any place where there's lots of evil, that makes power. You can feel it, can't you?'

A kind of warm wind stirred off the bare field under the one high light. Underhill shivered. Yes, even now, at midnight, the playground was evil, for it was used for evil things. 'Are all playgrounds like this?'

'Some. Maybe this is the only one like this. What I wanted to say is that Tom Marshall was like you. He worried about Tommy Marshall and the playground and the kids, too. He wanted to save Tommy the trouble and the hurt, also.'

This business of talking about people as if they were remote, made Mr. Underhill feel like laughing.

'So we made a bargain,' said the boy.

'Who with?'

'With the playground, I guess, or whoever runs it.'

'Who runs it?'

'I've never seen him. There's an office over there under the grandstand. A light burns in it all night. It's a bright, blue light, kind of funny. There's a desk there with no papers on it and an empty chair. The sign says Manager, but nobody ever sees the man.'

'He must be around.'

'That's right,' said the boy. 'Or I wouldn't be where I am, and someone else wouldn't be where they are.'

'You certainly talk grown-up.'

The boy was pleased. 'Want to know who I really am? I'm not Tommy Marshall. I'm Tom Marshall, the father. I know you won't believe it. But I was afraid for Tommy. I was the way you are now about Jim. So I made this deal with the playground. Oh, there are others, too. You'll see them among the kids.'

'You'd better run home to bed.'

'You want it to be true. I saw your eyes then! If you could trade places with Jim, you would. Save him all that torture, let him be in your place, grown-up, the real work over and done.'

'Any decent parent sympathizes with his children.'

'You more than most. You feel every kick. You come here tomorrow. You can make a deal, too.'

'Trade places?' It was an amusing, but an oddly satisfactory thought. 'What would I have to do?'

'Just make up your mind.' He tried to make it sound casual, a joke. But his mind was in a rage, again, frantic. 'What would I pay?'

'Nothing. You'd just have to play in the playground.'

'All day?'

'And go to school, of course.'

'And grow up again?'

'Yes. Be here at four.'

'I have work in the city tomorrow.'

'Tomorrow,' said the boy.

'You'd better get home to bed, Tommy.'

'My name is *Tom* Marshall,' said the boy, sitting there.

The playground lights went out.

Mr. Underhill and his wife did not speak at breakfast. He usually phoned her at noon to chat about this or that, but he did not phone. But at one-thirty, after a bad lunch, he dialled the house number. When Susan answered he hung up. Five minues later he phoned again.

'Charlie, was that you called five minutes ago?'

'Yes,' he said.

'I thought I heard you breathing before you hung up. What'd you call about, dear?' She was being sensible again.

'Oh, just called.'

'It's been a bad two days, hasn't it? You do see what I mean, don't you, Charlie? Jim must go to the playground and get a few scabs.'

'A few scabs, yes.'

He saw the blood and the hungry foxes and the torn rabbits.

'And learn to give and take,' she was saying, 'and fight if he has to.'

'Fight if he has to,' he murmured.

'I knew you'd come around.'

'Around,' he said. 'You're right. No way out. He must be sacrificed.'

'Oh, Charlie, you're so odd.'

He cleared his throat. 'Well, that's settled. Love me?'

'Yes.'

I wonder what it would be like, he thought.

'Miss me?' he asked the phone.

He thought of the diagrams in the dust, the boy seated there with the hidden bones in his face.

'Yes,' she said.

'I've been thinking,' he said. 'The playground.'

'Speak up.'

'I'll be home at three,' he said, slowly, piercing out the words, like a man hit in the stomach, gasping for breath. 'We'll take a walk, you and Jim and I,' he said, eyes shut.

'Wonderful!'

'To the playground,' he said and hung up.

It was really autumn now, the real chill, the real snap, the trees overnight burnt red and snapped free of their leaves, which spiralled about Mr. Underhill's face as he walked up the front steps, and there were Susan and Jim, bundled up because of the sharp wind, waiting for him.

'Hello!' they cried to one another, with much embracing and kissing. 'There's Jim down there!' 'There's Daddy up there!' They laughed and he felt paralysed and in terror of the late day. It was almost four. He looked at the leaden sky, which might pour down molten silver any moment, a sky of lava and soot and a wet wind blowing out of it. He held his wife's arm very tightly as they walked. 'Aren't you friendly, though?' She smiled.

'It's ridiculous, of course,' he said, thinking of something else.

'What?'

They were at the playground gate.

'Hello, Charlie. Hi!' Far away, atop the monstrous slide stood the Marshall boy, waving, not smiling now.

'You wait here,' said Mr. Underhill to his wife. 'I'll only be a moment. I'll just take Jim in.'

'All right.'

He grasped the small boy's hand. 'Here we go, Jim. Stick close to Daddy'

They stepped down the hard concrete steps and stood in the flat dust. Before them, in a magical sequence, stood diagrams, gigantic-tic-tac-toes, monstrous hopscotches, the amazing numerals and triangles and oblongs of children's scrabbling in the incredible dust.

The sky blew a huge wind upon him and he was shivering. He grasped the little boy's hand still tighter and turned to his wife. 'Good-bye!' he said. For he was believing it. He was in the playground and believing it, and it was for the best. Nothing was too good for Jim! Nothing at all in the crazy world! And now his wife was laughing back at him, 'Charlie, you idiot!'

They were running, running across the dirt playground floor, at the bottom of a stony sea that pressed and blew upon them. Now Jim was crying, 'Daddy, Daddy!' and the children racing to meet them, the boy on the slide yelling, the tic-tac-toe and hopscotches whirling, a sense of bodiless terror gripping him, but he knew what he must do and what must be done and what would happen. Far across the field footballs sailed, baseballs whizzed, bats flew, fists jabbed up, and the door of the Manager's office stood open, the desk empty, the seat empty, a lone light burning in it.

Mr. Underhill stumbled, shut his eyes and fell, crying out, his body clenched by a hot pain, mouthing strange words, everything in turmoil.

'There you are, Jim,' said a voice.

And he was climbing, climbing, eyes closed, climbing metal, ringing ladder rungs, screaming, wailing, his throat raw.

Mr. Underhill opened his eyes.

He was on top of the slide. The gigantic slide which was ten thousand feet high, it seemed. Children after him, children beating him to go on, slide! slide!

And he looked, and there, going off across the field, was a man in a black overcoat. And there, at the gate, was a woman waving and the man standing there with the woman, both of them looking in at him, waving, and their voices calling, 'Have a good time! Have a good time, Jim!'

He screamed. He looked at his hands, in a panic of realization. The small hands, the thin hands. He looked at the earth far below. He felt his nose bleeding and there was the Marshall boy next to him. 'Hi!' cried the other, and bashed him in the mouth. 'Only twelve years here!' cried the other in the uproar.

Twelve years! thought Mr. Underhill, trapped. And time is different to children. A year is like ten years. No, not twelve years of childhood ahead of him, but a century, a century of *this*!

'Slide!'

He was pinched, pummelled and shoved. He felt fists rising, he saw the fox faces, and beyond them, at the fence, the man and woman walking off. He screamed, he shrieked, he covered his face, he felt himself pushed, bleeding, to the rim of nothingness. Face first, he careened down the slide, screeching, with ten thousand monsters behind. A thought jumped through his brain a moment before he hit bottom in a nauseous mound of claws.

This is Hell, this is Hell!

And no one in the hot, milling heap contradicted him.

EPILOGUE

*It was almost midnight. The moon was high in the sky now.
The Illustrated Man lay motionless. I had seen what there was
to see. The stories were told; they were over and done.*

*There remained only that empty space upon the Illustrated
Man's back, that area of jumbled colours and shapes.*

*Now, as I watched, the vague patch began to assemble itself,
in slow dissolvings from one shape to another and still another.
And at last a face formed itself there, a face that gazed out at
me from the coloured flesh, a face with a familiar nose and
mouth, familiar eyes.*

*It was very hazy. I saw only enough of the Illustration to
make me leap up. I stood there in the moonlight, afraid that the
wind or the stars might move and wake the monstrous gallery at
my feet. But he slept on, quietly.*

*The picture on his back showed the Illustrated Man himself,
with his fingers about my neck, choking me to death. I didn't
wait for it to become clear and sharp and a definite picture.*

*I ran down the road in the moonlight. I didn't look back. A
small town lay ahead, dark and asleep. I knew that, long before
morning, I would reach the town. . . .*

Bestselling Transatlantic Fiction in Panther Books

THE SOT-WEED FACTOR	John Barth	£1·50 ☐
BEAUTIFUL LOSERS	Leonard Cohen	60p ☐
THE FAVOURITE GAME	Leonard Cohen	40p ☐
TARANTULA	Bob Dylan	50p ☐
MIDNIGHT COWBOY	James Leo Herlihy	35p ☐
LONESOME TRAVELLER	Jack Kerouac	35p ☐
DESOLATION ANGELS	Jack Kerouac	50p ☐
THE DHARMA BUMS	Jack Kerouac	40p ☐
BARBARY SHORE	Norman Mailer	40p ☐
AN AMERICAN DREAM	Norman Mailer	40p ☐
THE NAKED AND THE DEAD	Norman Mailer	60p ☐
THE BRAMBLE BUSH	Charles Mergendahl	40p ☐
TEN NORTH FREDERICK	John O'Hara	50p ☐
FROM THE TERRACE	John O'Hara	75p ☐
OURSELVES TO KNOW	John O'Hara	60p ☐
THE DICE MAN	Luke Rhinehart	95p ☐
COCKSURE	Mordecai Richler	60p ☐
ST. URBAIN'S HORSEMAN	Mordecai Richler	50p ☐
BLUE MOVIE	Terry Southern	60p ☐
THE CITY AND THE PILLAR	Gore Vidal	40p ☐
SLAUGHTERHOUSE 5	Kurt Vonnegut, Jr.	60p ☐
MOTHER NIGHT	Kurt Vonnegut, Jr.	40p ☐
PLAYER PIANO	Kurt Vonnegut, Jr.	50p ☐
GOD BLESS YOU, MR. ROSEWATER		
	Kurt Vonnegut, Jr.	50p ☐
WELCOME TO THE MONKEY HOUSE		
	Kurt Vonnegut, Jr.	40p ☐

All-action Fiction from Panther